Note to Readers

While the Allerton and Schmidt families are fictional, the flu epidemic of 1918–19 was all too real. More Americans died from that flu than died from fighting in World War I.

Other details in this story actually happened as well. The boys in Minneapolis started killing songbirds with their slingshots, so slingshots were made illegal and the schools had a bird day to teach children about the importance of birds.

The plane crash with Pilot Butters in downtown Minneapolis happened as well. Because of it, people started talking about creating laws that would limit how low planes could fly over cities.

When the flu epidemic was over and the soldiers returned from the war, people wanted to forget about all the difficult times they had been through. To this day, many history books don't even mention the Spanish flu that killed so many people throughout the world during the winter of 1918.

✯ *The* ✯ FLU EPIDEMIC

JoAnn A. Grote

BARBOUR
PUBLISHING, INC.
Uhrichsville, Ohio

ISBN 1-57748-451-7

Published by Barbour Publishing, Inc.
P.O. Box 719
Uhrichsville, Ohio 44683
http://www.barbourbooks.com

Printed in the United States of America.

Cover illustration by Peter Pagano.
Inside illustrations by Adam Wallenta.

CHAPTER 1

The Flu Strikes

Larry Allerton scowled at the small pieces of white gauze hanging from his mother's fingers. "Do we *have* to wear those masks again today?"

His mother smiled cheerfully. "You know your father's orders. As long as the flu epidemic lasts, we are to wear the masks whenever we leave the house and inside whenever we have company. He's a doctor, and he should know what is best for us. Isn't it better to wear the mask than catch the flu?"

"I'm not so sure." Larry snatched the thin mask from his mother. "None of my friends or the other Scouts have to wear them. I'm the only ten-year-old boy in the neighborhood who looks like he's playing Jesse James and the outlaws every time I go outside."

Mother and eight-year-old Gloria laughed.

Larry tied the strings of the mask behind his head while Gloria took her mask. "Larry is right," she said. "These things are nasty."

"Masks are nasty," five-year-old Harrison repeated. He shook his head back and forth while his mother tried to tie the strings of his mask without catching them in his straight, dark hair. Mother laughed softly at his antics, even though it took her a few tries to finish her chore.

She looked at her three children. "Does everyone have a jacket on? Good."

The sunlight coming in through the window in the door flashed on the pin on Mother's coat lapel. The pin was red. Yellow letters said, "Bread not beer." Larry couldn't remember when his mother and her suffragist friends hadn't been fighting for good things for women and families and against alcohol.

She frowned, looking about her. "Now, where did I put that basket? We don't want to forget your father's favorite cookies after each of you gave up sugar so he could have them."

"Here it is," Gloria said as she picked up the basket from the wooden bench in the hall. The basket was covered with a plain linen dishtowel.

Larry's mouth watered at the thought of the cookies in that basket. Because of the war, they hardly ever had desserts made with real sugar. But as of yesterday, the war was officially over. Larry didn't think he'd ever forget November 11, 1918, when the streets of Minneapolis had filled with people having a wild celebration over the end of the war.

Harry grabbed the edge of the basket, almost tipping it over. "Can I have a cookie?"

"No, Larry, I mean, Harry." Mother gently peeled his fingers from the basket. "These are for Father."

It seemed to Larry that Mother was always mixing up his and Harry's names. He supposed that was why she so often called them Lawrence and Harrison. He didn't mind that she mixed them up. Sometimes he even pretended not to hear her right. Like when she told him to stop doing something and he didn't want to stop. He'd just tell her that he thought she'd said Harry, not Larry.

Larry was glad Mother had kept a couple cookies out for each of them, but most were for Father. "To let him know how much we miss him while he's working so hard with the flu patients at the City Hospital," Mother had said.

Besides, he reminded himself, *the government has already said people can start using more sugar.*

"Now that the war's over, Harry, we'll soon be able to have as many sugar cookies as we can eat," he told his pouting brother.

Larry took his wide-brimmed Boy Scout hat from the hooks on the hall tree. He pulled it down over his strawberry-blond hair as far as it would go. He wished he could hide his whole face with his hat! Maybe then no one would know who he was in this silly mask.

As they left the house, he glanced across at the parlor window of his friend Jack Hasting's house across the street. It was always the first place he looked when he left the house. The small flag with the blue star was still in the window. Larry let out his breath in a quick sigh of relief. The flag hadn't been changed for one with a silver star, so Jack's brother, Greg, hadn't been reported wounded. The flag hadn't been changed for one with a gold star, so Greg hadn't been reported killed, either.

Greg was in France. He'd been fighting with the 151st in the Great War. But now the war was over! The soldiers would be coming home.

Doubt wiggled in Larry's chest. Jack's family hadn't heard from Greg for a few months. Greg could be somewhere in a hospital, wounded. Or a prisoner. Or dead, even, and the army just hadn't told the family yet.

Larry scowled. He tried to push the uncomfortable thoughts out of his mind. "Come on, Gloria! I'll race you to the corner!"

"Me, too!" Harry called.

It felt good to run, his shoes scrunching crisp fall leaves. The wind pushed at the wide brim of his hat and whipped the yellow Scout tie from beneath his open jacket. He was the first one to the corner, but Gloria was right behind him. Harry was only halfway there. Watching him, Larry laughed. Harry's legs and arms were pumping.

He stopped laughing when he saw a black wagon pulled by plodding horses coming down the street. Behind it was a car carrying a family all dressed in black. Some people were walking behind the car. The women were dressed in black. The men wore black armbands and black crepe around their hats.

"A funeral." Gloria's words were quiet.

"Horses!" Harry pointed. "I like horses."

"Shhh!" Larry grabbed Harry's hand, hiding the pointing finger. "It's a funeral. Be quiet."

Harry frowned. "Why must I be quiet, Larry?"

"Because somebody died."

"Died?"

Larry didn't know how to explain to a little boy what dead

meant. “Just be quiet,” he whispered.

The horse’s hooves thudded against the pavement, and the iron protecting the hearse’s wooden wheels rang out. The car chugging and jerking along behind seemed noisy compared to the boxlike wagon.

“Do you think the person died from the flu?” Gloria asked, looking at Larry over Harry’s head.

Larry shrugged. He hoped he didn’t look as nervous as he felt. “How should I know?”

Mother reached them as the last of the funeral procession passed their corner, and they hurried on.

“I don’t know how the horses and cars can make it through the streets,” Mother said. “Look at the mess the people left after celebrating the armistice signing last night!”

“It’s not that bad.” Larry looked around. There was a lot of stuff in the street and yards. Paper was everywhere. He saw an ash pail lying in the middle of the street. A milk can leaned against a tree on the boulevard, with a wooden spoon beside it.

Pails and milk cans made a great noise when you beat on them. He’d heard a lot of that the last couple nights! It must have been wonderful downtown, where people did snake dances down the street and through the stores.

Just remembering the last two nights made his heart beat faster. The news of the armistice had reached Minneapolis by wire at two o’clock in the morning. The city started celebrating and didn’t quit until late last night. “The wildest twenty-four hours in the history of Minneapolis,” the morning newspaper had said.

Gloria straightened her shoulders and set her mouth. Larry knew that look. He called it her “little mother” look. “Father said people are going to pay for getting together and celebrating that way. They'll catch the flu, and then they'll be sorry." Larry groaned. Gloria could be so prim! "They were only celebrating the greatest day the world has ever known. That's what the newspaper called it, anyway," he reminded her. "Besides, even Father said, 'It isn't everyday you can celebrate the end of a world war.' "

His sister propped her fists on her hips. "Well, Father still said—"

"That's enough bickering, children," Mother said. "You are both right."

At the next corner, they had to wait for another funeral procession to pass. It seemed to Larry he'd seen more funeral processions in the last few weeks since the flu epidemic started than he had in the whole rest of his life.

He didn't need funerals to remind him of the flu. This was Tuesday. If it weren't for the flu, he and Gloria would be in school right now. The schools had been closed for a month to keep children from catching and spreading the flu. At first, he'd thought it would be fun to have school closed. It hadn't ended up being as much fun as he'd hoped. There were lots of places they couldn't go and things they couldn't do because of the flu.

It's only because of Boy Scouts that I get out of the house at all, he thought. Even this morning, after they saw his father, he would be going to help distribute soup to people with the flu. His mother and Gloria and Harry would go to the dry goods store and the meat market and the grocery.

Because of the flu, ladies were supposed to do their shopping when men weren't going to and from work. Some of the city's leaders thought that way the trolleys wouldn't be as full and not as many people would catch the flu from each other.

At the next corner, they waited for a trolley to whiz past,

rocking on its tracks in the middle of the street. Paper scattered in the road from the night's celebration went flying as the trolley passed.

Through the open windows, they could hear people tooting horns and ringing cowbells. People on the trolley were singing the new version of "When Johnny Comes Marching Home." As they crossed the street, Larry started singing along, and Gloria chimed in:

Johnny is marching home again
He's finished another fight.
He's proved again the side he's on
Is ever and always right.
He won a war they thought was tied
And did it in record time.
Johnny is marching home again
So let the joy-bells chime.

"Can't we ride the trolley?" Harry asked. "I'm tired of walkin'."

Mother took his hand. "No, dear. The fresh air is good for us."

"She means we might catch the flu if we ride the trolley with all those other people," Larry told him.

His mother frowned at him and shook her head. He supposed she didn't want him to scare his little brother. *But everyone talks about the flu,* he thought.

He was about sick to death of hearing about the flu. The Old Spanish Lady, he and Jack called it. People called it the Spanish flu because they thought that was where it started.

His father said it didn't start in Spain, though. In the United

States, it seemed to have started in the army camps. Thousands of soldiers in the United States and Europe had died from it.

"Look!" Gloria pointed at the door of a small, white wooden house. A quarantine sign was posted to the door.

Larry knew what that meant. No one was to enter the house, and no one was to leave it. There were lots of doors with quarantine signs lately.

The house next door had a quarantine sign, too. Beneath it hung a large black crepe bow. That meant someone in the house had died, probably from the flu.

Gloria moved closer to him and touched his arm. "I'm glad no one we know has died from the flu, aren't you?" She spoke in a low voice so Harry couldn't hear.

"Of course." Larry shrugged off her hand. Her question made him uncomfortable. Lots of people had the flu—and there were a lot of people dying from it—but he couldn't believe anyone he knew could get that sick from a little flu bug. He'd had the flu before, last year. He'd had to miss a few days of school, and he'd thrown up and been sore, but it wasn't so bad.

"Look what I see!" Harry pulled his hand from his mother's. He raced toward the street and picked up a tin lunch pail. It was rusty and covered with dents.

"Someone must have used their lunch pail for a drum during the celebration last night," Larry told him.

Harry squatted down and picked up a stick. "I can drum, too." He began beating on the side of the pail. "Johnny comes marchin' home!" he sang, off key.

"Mercy, such a racket!" Mother grabbed the stick.

"No!" Harry hung on tight.

"You can play drum later," she told him, taking the stick away.

She glanced at Larry above Harry's head and rolled her eyes, but Larry saw she was grinning. She was always happy when they went to see Father.

Gloria fell into step beside Mother. "Do you think Father will come home with us today?"

"No, dear," Mother answered. "He has to help the flu patients. You know that."

Gloria's blue eyes looked sad. "But Father always used to come home at night when he was done helping patients."

"It's different this time." Mother put an arm around Gloria's shoulders, covering the girl's dark curls. "Remember what I told you before? With so many doctors and nurses over in Europe taking care of soldiers in the war, there aren't enough left here at home to help the flu patients. Sometimes Father only has time for a couple hours of sleep at night."

"Sometimes he doesn't get any sleep at all," Larry told Gloria. "There's nothing but flu patients on five floors of the hospital. The hospital can't take any more patients, 'cause they don't have enough people to take care of them."

Gloria scowled at him. "Father will come home for my birthday, won't he? It's only a couple weeks away."

Mother smiled at her and squeezed her shoulder. "I'm sure he will if he can. He hates being away from us as much as we hate him staying away. He is only staying with the other doctors in the house near the hospital to keep us safe from the flu. But just think how happy he is going to be when we give him these lovely cookies you helped bake!"

Gloria took the basket from her mother, carrying it with both hands. "I still wish he'd come home for my birthday."

They were almost at the large two-story white wooden house where their father was staying. Larry ran ahead, eager to see his father. Harry chased after him, the dented tin pail banging against his leg.

Larry felt a pang of disappointment in his chest. His father wasn't waiting for them on the wide porch like usual. Even when he was, they had to stay on the sidewalk and he stayed on the porch when they talked so they wouldn't catch the flu from him. Even that was better than not seeing him at all. Hadn't he been able to get away from the flu patients to see them today?

"Where's Father?" Harry asked. "I want to show him my drum!"

"I don't know," Larry answered.

When Mother and Gloria reached them, Larry could see the disappointment in their eyes. "Let's wait a few minutes," Mother suggested. "I know Father will try to get away from his patients to see us for a couple minutes."

The words were hardly out of her mouth before a young man wearing a gauze mask like the Allertons stepped out the front door onto the porch. Standing by the door, he called to Mother. "Are you Mrs. Allerton, by any chance?"

"Yes!"

"I'm sorry to tell you this, but Dr. Allerton can't visit with you today. He's caught the flu and is in bed with it."

Larry heard his mother gasp. He darted a look at her face. He'd never seen it so white. Her eyes were huge.

She took a deep breath. "May I see him?"

The young man shook his head. "I'm sorry, but no. We will have to quarantine this house."

"Of course," Mother said.

Larry didn't think the man could hear her. She hardly spoke above a whisper.

As they watched, the man nailed a quarantine sign on the door.

Larry gulped. Would there be a black crepe bow beneath that sign like the one they'd seen just a few blocks away?

Angry, he pushed the thought of the black bow out of his mind. His father was strong. The old flu wouldn't be strong enough to really hurt him!

Chapter 2
A Risky Project

Larry was still angry when he got off the trolley car at South Sixteenth Avenue on his Boy Scout assignment. Why did God let doctors get sick? They were supposed to help people! How could they help people if they got sick?

His mother hadn't liked letting him ride the trolley, but the Settlement House was too far from the hospital to walk. Mother had made him promise to sit in a seat by himself and next to an open window. It had been a cold ride.

The Pillsbury Settlement House rose high above him. It was a long wooden building. Like everywhere else in the city, there were signs of celebration scattered about the street and walk. A couple young ladies were gathering up paper from the walk and stuffing it into gunny sacks.

He smelled the soup before he even entered the building. His stomach growled. It reminded him of the cookies they'd brought for his father. His mother had taken them home. She'd said if Father had the flu, he wouldn't be wanting the cookies until he was well.

A truck with wooden rails on the back was parked in front of the building. A couple men were unloading vegetables. Larry's Scout leader had told the troop that people were donating vegetables to the Settlement House soup kitchens.

Inside, Larry hurried down the hall to the kitchen. A young lady brushed a stray lock of hair from her flushed face and smiled at him. "Another Boy Scout! Welcome! We're not quite ready to send the Scouts out with deliveries yet. Your friends are on the far side of the room." She pointed to them.

"Thank you." He made his way through the kitchen. He saw his best friend, Jack, waiting with the other Scouts.

The room was bustling with activity. At the stoves, women in aprons ladled soup from large black kettles into quart jars made of thick, clear glass. Heat from the large stoves made the kitchen feel good to Larry after his cold ride.

"Hi!" Jack grinned at him. "You're the last Scout to get here."

Mr. Jones, the balding, pudgy, middle-aged Scout leader, nodded a hello to Larry. Their troop used to have a younger leader, but he was off with the soldiers now.

Larry noticed all the other Scouts were carrying their

masks or letting them hang by their strings from one ear. In the blink of an eye, he slipped his mask down, too.

Mr. Jones held up a hand to get the Scouts' attention. "Let's go over what we're doing today. As you know, these fine ladies are making soup for people whose families have influenza. If their houses are under quarantine, they can't go out and buy their own food. Sometimes there isn't anyone in the house who is strong enough to cook. What you Scouts are doing today is very important."

Larry glanced at Jack and tried not to smile. He shrugged nervously as one corner of Jack's mouth lifted in a smile. It felt good to be doing something to help other people. He was a little embarrassed at feeling proud of it.

"Remember the rules of flu safety," Mr. Jones continued. "What is the first rule?" He held the index finger of one hand against the small finger of his other hand, counting.

"Always wear your mask over your nose and mouth." Larry repeated the rule aloud along with the rest of the Scouts.

Mr. Jones moved to the next finger. "Second rule?"

"Don't go in anyone's house."

"Good." Mr. Jones moved another finger. "What should you do after you knock?"

"Set the soup down beside the door and move back to the sidewalk."

"Last rule?" Mr. Jones's eyebrows lifted until they were hidden beneath the brim of his Boy Scout hat.

"Stick with your buddy."

Mr. Jones settled his hands on his hips and nodded. "Sounds like you're all set."

The ladies who had made the soup handed each of the boys a large basket filled with a number of jars of soup. Also there was a list of addresses with the number of jars to leave at each address.

When a lady held a basket out to Larry, he pointed to Jack. "We're buddies. Can we have baskets that go to houses near each other?"

"Of course," she said, taking a quick look at the addresses in Larry's basket.

Larry took the handle of his basket and blinked in surprise. It was heavier than he'd expected! He didn't want to have to carry it with two hands. With a grunt, he leaned to the other side to make it easier to carry. Jack soon had his basket, and the two boys left the building.

Outside, Larry was surprised to see Uncle Erik jump off the trolley. He strode briskly down the sidewalk toward the Settlement House, a camera in his hand. His hat was tipped a little to one side, like usual.

Uncle Erik stopped in front of Larry and Jack, a big grin on his face. "My editor sent me here to cover a story about Boy Scouts delivering soup for the Settlement House to influenza victims. I didn't know you two were going to be in the troop making the deliveries. How about if I take your picture for the paper?"

Larry pushed his shoulders back and tried to stand straighter when Uncle Erik pointed his big black camera at them. He grinned until his cheeks hurt.

When Uncle Erik went inside, Jack smiled his one-sided smile at Larry. "Wow! We're goin' to be in the newspaper! Who woulda thought?"

Larry grinned back and set his basket on the sidewalk. He picked up the list of addresses from his basket. "Let's see where we're supposed to go."

They looked over their lists together. A couple minutes later they'd figured out the quickest way to the houses and started off.

As the two boys walked along the streets near the Mississippi River, Larry studied the houses curiously. They weren't in the best part of town. A lot of immigrants from Sweden and Norway lived here, and they did not have much money.

Larry switched his basket from one hand to the other. "My father said he was afraid lots of people in this part of town would catch the flu," he told Jack. "Lots of them can't read English, and some can't speak it very well. Father said they might not be able to read the flu safety rules in the newspaper and on the posters around town."

The first stop was at a small wooden house. Almost all the paint had peeled off the walls.

Larry glanced at his list. "It says an old man lives here by himself."

There was a quarantine sign on the door, but Larry and Jack had expected that. All the people on the soup list had been reported by visiting nurses. Probably the nurses had put the sign on the door. Larry knew from his father that people didn't usually put quarantine signs on their doors unless a doctor or nurse visited them. Lots of sick people didn't get a visit from a doctor or nurse because there weren't enough doctors and nurses to see everyone.

Larry knocked on the door beneath the quarantine sign. He set a jar of soup down and moved back to the sidewalk beside Jack. After a couple minutes, no one had come to the door.

"Do you suppose he's dead?" Jack whispered.

The hair on the back of Larry's neck rose, like it did when

some of the Scouts told ghost stories. "Why are you whispering?"

Jack cleared his throat. "Well, do you think he is?"

Larry was glad he spoke louder this time. "Likely he's just too sick to come to the door. We'd better tell the ladies at the Settlement House when we get back. They can send a nurse to check on him."

He tried to ignore the picture Jack's question had brought into his imagination as they moved on to the next house on his list.

"My list says to leave four jars of soup here. There's a family of seven in this house, and they all have the flu."

A boy about their own age came to the door to get the bottles Larry and Jack had left on the porch. He looked very tired. His shirt was wet, like he'd been sweating a lot. He lifted a thin hand in a wave. "Thanks."

Larry could hardly hear him.

Now that Larry's basket was empty, he took a couple jars from Jack's basket and put them in his own. For the next house on the list, they had to go down a long flight of wooden steps. The steps took the boys from the ridge above the river to a group of small houses beside the river. The November breeze seemed chillier down by the water. Larry liked the smell of the river.

They only had to leave one bottle of soup at each of the first two houses on Jack's list. Larry was relieved when someone came to the door to get the bottles both times.

The last house on the list was gray and weathered looking from years of standing near the river. A long, narrow porch with a rickety railing covered the front of the house. Larry's heart jumped to his throat when he saw the black bow beneath the quarantine sign.

Jack glanced at his list. Then he looked at Larry with big

eyes. "It doesn't say anything here about anybody being dead."

Larry swallowed the lump in his throat. "You're whispering again."

"So are you."

Angry at himself, Larry tried to speak a little louder. "There are probably people who need soup inside, even if someone in the house d. . .died." He gave Jack a little shove. "Go on."

Jack walked slowly toward the house. Larry was glad this house was on Jack's list and not his!

Jack set down two bottles of soup and knocked on the door. He all but ran back to Larry.

The door opened. A young woman in a black dress looked out at them. "Yah? What can I do for you?" she asked in a Swedish accent.

Larry could hear crying coming from inside the house. He took a step back.

Jack gulped and pointed to the bottles. "We brought soup from the Settlement House."

The woman looked slowly from them to the bottles. *"Tak."*

Larry knew that meant *thank you.* He and Jack hurried away. He was glad to leave that sad house behind.

When they got back to the Settlement House, Larry told one of the ladies about the man who didn't come to his door. Jack told her about the house with the black bow on the door.

"Let's go to the park," Jack said when they left the Settlement House.

Larry knew his mother expected him to go straight home, but he went with Jack anyway. When Jack took off his mask and stuck it in his pocket, Larry did the same. He tried to ignore the guilty feeling in his chest.

They'd barely reached the park before Jack pulled out a slingshot.

"Hey, when did you get that?" Larry asked.

"Bought it yesterday," Jack said with a bit of a swagger.

"It's a beauty."

Larry watched in admiration as Jack picked up a small stone, took aim at a twig, pulled back the rubber sling, and let go. The twig broke from the branch with a sharp snap.

"Good shot."

"Say, there's a squirrel!" Jack picked up a pebble and took aim at the chattering animal sitting on a branch six feet above the ground.

"Hey!" Larry grabbed his arm. "Don't shoot him!"

Jack scowled but lowered his slingshot. "It's just a squirrel. Me and some other friends were in the park near home the other day, and we killed lots of birds."

Larry stared at him. "Why?"

Jack shrugged. "Why not? In the war, men killed other men, didn't they? How do you learn to shoot and kill things if you don't practice? What's the matter with killing a few birds and squirrels?"

"I–I don't know. I just never killed anything before. Not on purpose. Except bugs."

Jack held out his slingshot. "Want to try to hit something?"

"Sure!"

Larry didn't aim at the squirrel, which had scurried to the ground and was busy looking beneath dead autumn leaves for nuts. He chose a twig with a lone brown maple leaf dangling from the end of it. He picked up a pebble. Then he took careful aim. He held his breath as he slowly pulled the rubber sling back.

Whiz! The stone flew threw the air. The slingshot vibrated in his hand.

"Missed!" Disappointment filled his voice. It had looked so easy when Jack shot.

"Takes a little practice. Try again. Maybe try for something a little larger."

This time Larry aimed at the maple leaf instead of the twig.

Whiz! The stone tore part of the leaf from the twig, leaving behind only a jagged edge.

"I did it!"

He tried again for the twig. Missed. "Oh, well." He handed the slingshot back to Jack.

"You'll get the hang of it with a little practice. Why don't you get a slingshot of your own? All the rest of the Scouts are getting them."

They were almost at the edge of the park when Jack aimed at something again. Before Larry could even see what his friend was shooting at, the pebble found its mark. A cardinal dropped to the ground.

Larry could see in a flash it was dead. His stomach tightened. "Why did you do that?"

Jack pushed at the dead bird with the tip of his toe. "I just felt like it." He stuffed his slingshot in his large coat pocket and grinned at Larry. "I'm going to make a great soldier one day."

Larry stared at the bird that had been so happily alive a minute earlier. "There aren't going to be any more wars, remember? That's what everyone says. This world war is supposed to be the end of war forever. We won't need more soldiers."

Jack shrugged. "You never know. If we do need soldiers, I'll be ready."

CHAPTER 3
Who's Next?

Larry put his hands behind his head, leaned back against the cool earth and sighed. A few feet below him, the Mississippi River flowed along on its way through the lower states to the Gulf of Mexico. He liked the smell of the river and moist earth and the musty smell of fallen leaves.

Jack dropped down beside him and rested his elbows on his knees. "Sure beats school all to thunder, doesn't it?"

"Sure does," Larry agreed.

It had been a great morning. The YMCA had planned activities for boys who were out of school because of the flu scare. They had joined a lot of other boys for a hike out along the Mississippi River. They'd had footraces and leapfrog contests and a pole vaulting contest.

Larry smiled to himself. He and Jack had tied for first place in the pole vaulting contest. It had felt good to do so well.

With a niggle of guilt, Larry remembered his mask. It was stuffed in one of his trouser pockets. His father didn't care what other people believed. He thought the masks should be worn by everyone, everywhere. He wasn't the only person who thought so. Some cities like San Francisco had made it a crime to be in public places without wearing a mask!

Out here along the river, a fellow could almost forget there was a flu epidemic or soldiers still in Europe, Larry thought. "Have you heard anything from Greg yet?" he asked Jack.

"Nope." Jack picked up a twig and tossed it into the river. Larry raised himself onto his elbows. Together he and Jack watched the current carry the twig away.

"How is your father?" Jack asked. "Is he over the flu yet?"

"Nope." Larry didn't want to think about his father. *He should have been getting better by now,* he thought. He took a deep breath, stretching his arms above his head, trying to get rid of the tight feeling in his chest.

Jack looked around, his eyebrows raised. "See the man from the YMCA anywhere?"

Larry glanced about. "No. He's probably putting out the campfire. That was some lunch, huh!" Food never tasted better to Larry than when cooked outdoors over a campfire.

The boys had each brought their own plate, cup, and fork. "Just like the soldiers," the leader had told them. Larry remembered seeing a picture of soldiers at camp. The soldiers were standing in line for lunch, each carrying their own plate and cup.

Jack was digging his slingshot out of his pocket.

"Hey!" Larry sat up with a start. "You aren't going to shoot any birds or anything, are you? Not here! The leader might get mad."

"Watch out for him for me, will you?" Jack slid farther down the bank, dead leaves crackling as he went.

Larry glanced about quickly, looking for the leader.

"Rats!" he heard Jack say. "Missed."

Larry was glad to hear it but didn't say so.

A moment later there was a thunk. Then, "Almost."

Larry glanced down at where his friend was squatting in the long, dead grass beside the river. At the sound of running feet, he looked back over the ridge. One of the other boys was coming toward them.

Larry jumped up. The boy waved an arm at him. "Come on! We're gettin' together a football game!"

"Be right there!" Larry called back. "Hey, Jack, let's go."

Jack stuffed his slingshot into his coat pocket and climbed up the bank.

"Get anything?" Larry asked.

"Nope. Would have on the next shot, though."

It was almost dinnertime when they reached home. Gloria and her best friend, Mabel, were jumping rope on the sidewalk outside the white picket fence that bordered the Allertons' front lawn. Mabel lived across the street in the house beside Jack. Her sister, Violet, was engaged to Jack's brother, Greg. Violet was also a good friend of Larry and Gloria's cousin, Lydia Schmidt.

The girls' knee-length corduroy skirts flapped as they jumped. Mabel's shoulder-length red curls and Gloria's fashionable short bob bounced in time with their jumps.

"Hi!" Gloria quit spinning her rope and ran over to the boys. Her blue eyes sparked with curiosity. "Did you have a good time?"

Larry grinned. "We had a *great* time!"

"Yep," Jack agreed.

"What did you do?" Gloria asked.

Larry told her about their day.

The corners of Gloria's mouth turned down in a pout. She crossed her arms over her chest. "I wish someone would arrange a day like that for girls. Boys aren't the only ones who get bored with school closed."

Jack stuck his hands in his trouser pockets and smiled his one-sided smile. "They didn't plan this because boys are bored. They planned it because they think it will keep boys out of trouble."

Gloria spread her hands, palms up. "Don't they want to keep girls out of trouble?"

Larry and Jack laughed. "Girls don't get into the kind of trouble boys get into," Larry said, feeling very grown up next to Gloria.

"That's right," Jack said. "When was the last time you heard of a girl throwing tomatoes at a building or breaking a window with a shot from her BB gun or slingshot?"

Gloria didn't laugh. "It's not fair that boys get to have more fun because they do more mean things than girls."

"Gloria's right." Mabel's freckled face was as angry as Gloria's.

The boys just laughed. "Too bad you weren't born boys

instead of girls!" Jack said. "See you later, Larry."

Larry headed straight for the kitchen. "Mother, I'm home!" he called, pushing open the dark, swinging door between the hall and the kitchen. His mouth watered at the smell of a roast cooking in the big white enamel oven.

The oven had warmed the kitchen. Larry thought the warm air felt good. The city health director warned everyone to leave windows cracked open in every room in the house. *The more fresh air, the less chance for people to catch the Old Spanish Lady,* he thought.

Larry's mother was on the telephone. She stood beside the large wooden box where it hung on the wall. She held a black cone-shaped piece of metal to her ear.

"Oh, Anna, that's just awful!" she said, speaking into the black cone-shaped mouthpiece attached to the wooden phone box.

"What's awful?" Larry whispered from beside her, realizing that his mother was probably talking with Aunt Anna.

She held a finger to her lips to warn him not to talk. "Will they let you see her?" she asked Aunt Anna.

Larry stopped listening and opened the door of the white wooden cabinet. He pulled the top off the cookie jar and stuck in a hand. A moment later, he pulled it out empty. Some of the sugar cookies Mother and Gloria had baked Father were still in the jar. Larry hadn't been able to eat any of them. Somehow they didn't taste good, knowing they were for Father and he was too sick to eat any.

Mother hung the earpiece on its hook with a sigh. "That was your aunt Anna."

"What's wrong?" Larry asked, looking through the cupboard and hoping to find something to snack on before dinner.

"Your cousin Lydia is sick. Violet, too."

Larry's hand froze on the shelf. He turned his head slowly to look at Mother. "Do they have the flu?"

"Yes." A troubled frown marked her usually cheerful face. "Did you know they both took a short course in nursing at the University of Minnesota?"

He nodded. Everyone knew there was a terrible shortage of nurses. Lots of nurses had gone to army camps or Europe to care for wounded soldiers. The army was always asking for more nurses. With the flu epidemic, there weren't enough nurses to help with all the sick people at home. The university had started a special short course in nursing to help train women. It only lasted a few months. Father had said, "They can't learn much in such a short time, but anything they learn will help."

Mother sighed. "Well, they've been helping nurse the soldiers at Fort Snelling. And they both came down with the flu!"

Larry's skin felt suddenly cold.

Mother opened the door of the oven and lifted the cover of a black Dutch oven with a pot holder. Hot air filled with the smell of roast beef and cooking vegetables poured through the kitchen.

It didn't smell as good to Larry as it had when he'd come home.

"The roast still has a little while to cook." She closed the oven door. Reaching behind her, she untied the sash of the printed apron that covered almost all of her house dress. "I'd best go over and tell Violet's mother that the girls are taken ill."

With one hand on the swinging door, she turned back to him. "I almost forgot to ask how your hike went."

"Fine. It was fine."

She smiled. "Good. You can tell me all about it over dinner."

"Yes."

Larry wandered out into the parlor. From one of the front windows, he watched his mother hurry down their front walk, through the white wooden gate, and across the street to Mabel's house.

Through the open window, he could hear Gloria and Mabel's jump ropes make a soft *klish* sound as they struck the sidewalk. In a singsong voice, the girls repeated a jumping-rope rhyme:

"I had a little bird.
Its name was Enza.
I opened up the window
And in-flew-Enza."

Larry slammed the window shut.

CHAPTER 4
More Warnings

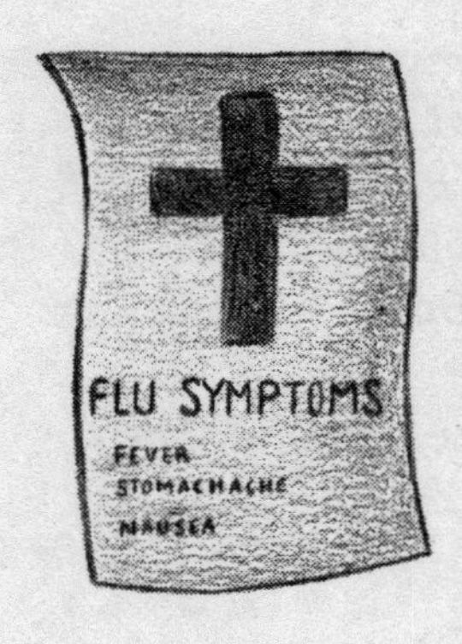

Larry swayed with the movement of the trolley car as it raced down the middle of the street toward downtown Minneapolis on Saturday. Through the open windows, he could hear the wheels clacking against the tracks.

From across the aisle, Jack grinned and pointed to a man a couple seats ahead of him. The man looked like he was taking a nap. His head rolled to the right, then back to the left, then to the right again. His hat perched precariously against the front of his head.

Larry grinned back at Jack. He wondered how the man kept that old hat from falling when he was asleep!

He wished he and Jack could sit next to each other so they

could talk more easily, but that was against the rules. Usually as many people as possible crowded onto trolley cars. Because of the flu, only one person was supposed to sit on each seat, and there was supposed to be an empty seat between each person.

Guilt squiggled through him. Mother wouldn't like it if she knew he was riding a trolley. He was only supposed to ride them if he didn't have any other choice. But he was so tired of walking everywhere! And he didn't want Jack to think he was a sissy.

Besides, he was bored! Not only were schools closed but churches and theaters and almost any place where people went for fun. His mother's women's suffrage meetings had been canceled—even the state suffrage rally. High school and college football games had been canceled. Boy Scout meetings had been canceled except when they were helping with war or flu efforts.

So when Jack said, "Let's ride the trolley downtown," Larry had agreed without thinking about it twice.

I need to buy a birthday present for Gloria, anyway, he thought. *How can I do that if I don't go shopping?*

The trolley stopped at a corner. Some passengers got off and others got on. A man forgot the rule and sat in a seat beside another man. He was quickly reminded to change seats.

Posters made up by the Red Cross were mounted above the windows. They told what to do to keep from getting the flu, how you could tell if you caught the flu, and what to do if you caught it. Larry and Jack and other Boy Scouts had helped the Red Cross deliver those posters to trolleys and businesses.

He read the list of ways to keep from catching the flu:

1. Work in a cool place with fresh air.
2. Walk rather than ride.

3. Ride in open air vehicles or with windows open.
4. Sleep with open windows.
5. Avoid large groups of people.
6. Wear a mask when with other people.

Larry shifted uncomfortably on the trolley seat. He was breaking two of those rules right now: riding instead of walking and not wearing his mask.

To put his guilt out of his mind, he read the next poster, "How to tell if you have the Spanish flu":

1. Muscles suddenly weak or aching.
2. Headache.
3. Fever for 3 to 5 days.
4. Within 2 days after fever leaves, cough appears.

The last poster said, "What to do if you catch the Spanish flu":

1. Go to bed at once.
2. Sleep in a room with open windows.
3. Call a doctor if:
a. you have a fever
b. you cough up pink sputum
c. breathing is fast and painful
4. Eat light foods.

Larry snorted. *I don't know why I'm bothering to read these. I know them all by heart!*

The trolley had reached downtown. At the next stop, Larry and Jack got off.

They walked up the sidewalk in front of large store windows and stopped in front of a window with a display of "the latest American-made toys for Christmas."

"I heard a lot of toys used to be made in Germany," Larry told Jack, "but no one in America wants to buy toys made there since the war started!"

There were lots of toy rifles and army hats just like soldiers carried and wore. But what caught Larry's eye was a slingshot—the best looking one he'd seen. He was the only guy among his friends without one. In a flash, he made up his mind. "I'm going to see how much that slingshot costs."

A clerk took the slingshot from the window and handed it to Larry. "It's the best one we sell. We just got it in two days ago."

A smile slipped over Larry's face. The handle of the slingshot fit his hand perfectly. It was made of wood. It had been polished until it shined like glass and was as smooth as a new marble.

"Wow! That's the best looking sling I've seen!" Jack's eyes were huge. "Beats mine all to."

Larry looked up at the tall skinny clerk. "How much is it?"

When he heard the price, he swallowed hard. It was a lot more than he'd thought it would be. He stared at the slingshot in his hands, biting his bottom lip. Should he buy it or not?

Jack nudged him with his elbow. "What's the matter? Cat got your tongue? Don't you have enough money?"

Larry shrugged. "I have enough." He didn't want to admit in front of the clerk that if he bought the slingshot, he might not be able to buy a present for Gloria.

"Then get it!" Jack urged. "You're not going to find a better one."

Larry took a deep breath and looked at the clerk. "I'll take it."

I'll have to figure out a way to earn more money before Gloria's birthday.

Walking along the downtown sidewalk a few minutes later, Larry and Jack hardly noticed that people had to walk around them. They were too busy admiring the new slingshot.

That's probably why Larry bumped into the man.

"Hey, watch where you're going!" The man scowled down at them.

"Sorry." Larry felt his face grow red.

"First flicker, one o'clock!"

Larry looked at the theater worker in surprise. Behind the worker, the doors to the movie theater stood wide open, even though it was the middle of November. People were hurrying inside. Other people were stopping to point at the poster set up on a board outside telling about the movie at one o'clock.

"I thought all the theaters were closed," he said to the theater clerk.

"They were. City health director said this morning that all the theaters can open this afternoon. Why don't you buy a ticket and see the show?"

"Let's do it!" Jack's eyes sparkled.

Larry bit his lip. "I don't have enough money along." He held out his slingshot. "I spent most of it on this."

"I'll loan you some."

Larry didn't say anything. He wanted to go to the movie, but if he borrowed money from Jack, he'd have to earn enough to pay him back *and* buy Gloria's present. Oh, well. He'd saved most of his spending from the money Mother gave him for school supplies. He'd make his pencils and erasers and paper last as long as he could so he could keep some of the money.

Jack nudged him. "What's the matter with you? The flickers

have been closed for five weeks! Don't you want to see the show?"

Larry nodded. He shoved his new slingshot into his coat pocket. "All right."

Larry was glad he went. The flicker was a comedy. It felt good to laugh long and hard at something again!

It would have been more fun if we could have sat together, he thought when they left the theater. Because of the flu, people had to sit every other seat while they watched the flicker. Just like on the trolley. *Stupid Old Spanish Lady!*

Two days later, on Monday, Larry woke up excited. His first thought was, *We get to go back to school today!*

The Sunday newspapers had told the city the worst of the flu epidemic was over. Time for the city to get back to normal.

Larry's second thought wasn't as cheerful. *I wish Father were over the flu.* Just because there weren't as many new cases of Spanish flu being reported didn't mean there weren't still a lot of sick people in the city.

After breakfast, Larry and Gloria hurried across the street like they did every school day. They always stopped at Jack's house and Mabel's house to pick up their friends. Larry saw with relief the small flag with the blue star was still in Jack's window.

Larry, Gloria, and Jack turned up the sidewalk to Mabel's house. Gloria stopped so suddenly that Larry stepped on the back of her shoes. "Hey, get moving!"

She didn't budge. She just pointed at the door. Her blue eyes were wide. Her pale skin was almost white.

Larry looked at the door. A quarantine sign! His stomach felt like someone had thrown a steel ball at it.

It seemed to Larry that the three of them stood staring at

that sign for a long time. Finally he turned and started toward school. Gloria and Jack followed. They all knew it was no use to stop for Mabel. Even if Mabel didn't have the flu, she wouldn't be allowed to leave the house.

It didn't make them feel any better when they had to stop to wait for a funeral procession to pass before crossing the next street.

By the time they were almost to school, the three were excited again. They talked about the friends they hadn't seen while school was closed.

"I want to see Elsie," Gloria told the boys, "and Lulu. They are my two best friends, next to Mabel."

Larry knew how she felt. Jack was his best friend, and he liked most of the other Boy Scouts, but there were other kids he liked playing and studying with at school. Wilbur was one of his favorites. Good old Will was a whiz at math. He always knew how to make any math problem seem easy. Larry didn't know how he'd get through some of the math lessons without Will!

When they reached school, Larry was surprised that no one was in the classrooms. Instead, everyone stood in a long, long line in the hallway.

"What's going on?" he asked the last student in line.

"The school nurse has to check everyone to be sure they don't have the flu before we can go to our classrooms."

"That will take all day!" Larry couldn't believe it. There was only one nurse for the whole school. How could she check out everyone?

But she managed. Larry found out she didn't do it all by herself after all. Teachers asked the students waiting in line some of the questions for the nurse. "Do you have a headache? Do you feel sore? Have you had a fever? Do you have a cough? Does anyone at your house have the flu? Has anyone at your house gotten over the flu in the last couple days?" they asked.

The nurse felt their foreheads to see whether they had a fever. If anyone felt warm, she would take their temperature.

Jack grinned his lopsided grin at Larry. "I almost wish I didn't feel good so the nurse would take my temperature. That would be fun!"

Larry shrugged. "Oh, it's not such a big deal." He and Gloria had had their temperatures taken often over the years. Only doctors and nurses had thermometers, so many of their friends had never had their temperatures taken.

A couple children were sent home from school. One of them was Gloria's friend, Elsie. Her cheeks were red from fever when she passed them.

"Hi, Elsie!" Gloria called to her, waving.

Elsie waved back weakly. She didn't smile.

A couple hours later, everyone had been checked by the nurse and classes started. The rooms were cold because a window was open in each room. The teacher in Larry's class had a hard time getting the students to quiet down. After all, they hadn't seen each other for five weeks!

"Before we get to our regular class," the teacher said when everyone was finally seated, "we're going to go over the rules of good sanitation."

Everyone groaned. Then they laughed at themselves because they'd all groaned at once.

The teacher held up a hand. "After all, we don't want to catch the flu, do we?"

The rules were listed on the blackboard. Most of the rules on the poster in the trolley were listed, but there were others, too: Don't spit. (Larry knew that was a new city law because of the flu.) Wash your hands before you eat. If you have to sneeze or cough, always sneeze or cough into a handkerchief. Don't touch things other people touch.

Larry thought it was the strangest school day of his life. He couldn't seem to remember what they had been studying in any topic when school had closed five weeks ago!

He was disappointed that his friend Wilbur wasn't in school. At first, Larry thought Wilbur must have the flu. Then he found out students were missing from class for a lot of reasons.

Some of the students had been kept home because their parents didn't want them around other students, where they might catch the flu. Some were out because other people in their family had the flu.

Finally he asked Miss Wilson if she knew why Wilbur wasn't in school. She placed a hand on his shoulder. "Wilbur won't be going to school here anymore. His mother died of the flu. His father can't take care of Wilbur and all his brothers and sisters by himself, so Wilbur and the others have been sent to foster homes."

Chills ran down Larry's spine. That Old Spanish Lady had taken Wilbur's mother and taken Wilbur away from his father and brothers and sisters!

He looked at every empty seat in the classroom, remembering who used to sit in each. Was that boy sick? Were his parents sick? Had his parents died? Would the boy ever be back in class?

Fear crawled along Larry's nerves. If Wilbur's mother could die from the flu, maybe Father could die from it, too!

He'd always thought his father was safe from really bad sickness. After all, he was a doctor. He always worked with sick people. God wouldn't let a doctor die, would He?

Would He?

Chapter 5
Gloria's Birthday

When Larry and Gloria got home from school, the first thing Larry did was ask his mother, "Did you see Father today?"

She shook her head, her lips pressed tightly together. "No. I went over to the house, but they still won't let me see him. He still has the flu."

Gloria put her arms around her mother's waist and hugged her. "Father will be better in time for my birthday, won't he?"

Larry frowned. Gloria's birthday was at the end of the week.

"I hope so, dear," Mother answered Gloria. "If he can't be here, we'll know he is with us in his heart."

Larry's stomach tightened. What if Father died like Wilbur's mother? What if he died and never came home again for any of their birthdays, or Thanksgiving, or Christmas, or anything else?

"Stupid old flu!" Gloria's voice was filled with anger. She still hugged her mother tightly. "Father wasn't supposed to catch the flu. He was helping people get better, wasn't he?"

"Yes." Mother's eyes filled with tears.

"I want him home!" Gloria let go of her mother and stomped her foot. "I don't want him to be a doctor anymore!"

"You don't mean that, dear." Mother stared at her with sad eyes.

"I do, too!"

Mother blinked away her own tears. "Father wants to help sick people."

Gloria stomped about the room. "Sick people keep him away from us. I don't want him to help them anymore!"

Mother caught Gloria's hands, making her stop. "What would sick people do if there weren't any doctors? Who would take care of them?"

Gloria tugged her hands away and crossed her arms over her chest. "I don't know, and I don't care!"

Larry tried to change the subject. "There's a quarantine sign on Mabel's door, Mother. We saw it when we went to pick her up for school this morning."

"I know. I brought soup and oranges over to their house and left them on the porch."

Just like the Boy Scouts, Larry thought.

When Gloria had finally gone up to her room, Larry asked his mother, "How can I earn some more money?"

"What do you need it for?"

"Well, Christmas is coming soon." That wasn't the whole truth, but it was part of the truth. Did telling only part of the truth count as telling the truth or telling a lie?

Mother thought a moment. "With your father away so much because of the flu, you have been more help than usual around the house and yard. I believe you deserve a little money for the help you've given me in the weeks since Father began working such long hours at the hospital."

She was so nice about it that Larry *almost* decided to tell her the *whole* truth about the reason he needed the money. Not that he'd done anything wrong, not truly wrong. He'd never been told he couldn't buy a slingshot or that he couldn't spend his money on that instead of Gloria's present.

Of course, Mother might be disappointed to know he had spent money on himself instead of buying his sister a gift. Selfish, she'd call it. And she wouldn't like it that he'd borrowed money from a friend, even though he was willing to work to pay the money back. Perhaps he'd better say nothing.

Because Mother was so nice about the money and because he felt so guilty about not telling the whole truth, Larry worked harder than ever at his chores that week.

It was a strange week.

"Every morning we have to stand in line and wait for the nurse to say we don't have the flu and can go to class," Larry complained to his mother on Friday at breakfast.

Mother spooned more hot oatmeal into his empty bowl. "The nurse only wants to be sure no one is spreading the flu to other children. It's for your own good."

"Why are things that are for our own good no fun?"

Mother's bubbly laugh was his only answer.

Every day that week, the first thing he asked when he got home from school was, "Did you see Father? Is he better yet?" The answer to both questions was always no.

It seemed like the questions about Father were always on

Larry's mind—when he played, when he was at school, and when he did his chores.

Is this what it's like for Jack? he wondered. *Does he worry about his brother Greg like this all the time?* It wasn't a good feeling!

There was some good news that week. The soldiers in camps in the United States had begun to be released now that the war was over. It would be a while before soldiers overseas came home.

"Did you read about this airplane?" Larry asked his mother eagerly one night, looking at her over the top of the Minneapolis *Tribune.* "It says here the plane carried twenty-five people over Paris, all at the same time! That must be a *huge* plane!"

"Twenty-five!" Mother stopped her mending to stare at him. "Are you sure you read it right? That's a lot of people."

"That's what it says: twenty-five people." Larry read the short article a dozen times.

One day, he promised himself, *I'm going to fly.*

Father didn't make it home for Gloria's birthday.

"She is going to be so disappointed," Mother told Larry. "Help me make it a special birthday for her anyway, won't you?"

Larry promised he would. He was sure she would like the present he'd chosen for her ninth birthday! He could hardly wait to give it to her.

Because it was Gloria's birthday, Mother made her favorite foods for dinner. They ate in the dining room and used Mother's best crystal and china. Mother even lit the candles in crystal holders in the middle of the table, just like she did when she and Father had special company. There was a beautiful birthday cake for dessert.

"This is the best cake I've ever had," Larry said. He scraped the last bit off his plate then held it out to his mother. "Can I have more? Please?"

"Me, too!" Harry held up his plate.

"I think I'll have another piece, too." Mother took their plates and stood up. "What about the birthday girl?"

Gloria shrugged. She still had a couple bites of cake left on her plate.

"It really is the best cake I've ever had. Don't you think so, Gloria?" Larry asked.

She shrugged again and pushed a small piece of cake around on her plate with her fork.

Mother set another piece of cake in front of each of the boys. "It probably is the best cake you've had since before the war. It's easier to make a cake that tastes like it should when there's plenty of flour and sugar. Now that the war is over, there are no more wheatless days. We are allowed to have more sugar, too."

Larry laughed. "Hey, Gloria, maybe the war ended when it did just so you could have a good birthday cake. What do you think?"

Gloria giggled, just a little. "I wish Father could have some of my birthday cake."

No one said anything for a minute.

Gloria looked at Mother. "Could we take Father a piece of my cake tomorrow?"

Mother shook her head. "Father can't eat cake when he has the flu."

Mother's eyes looked sad. Larry hated to see her eyes look that way. When Father was home with them, Mother was almost always cheerful. She used to sing while she worked in the kitchen or cleaned house. He couldn't remember hearing her sing since Father caught the flu.

Helping with dishes was usually Gloria's chore, but Larry helped that night. "Only because it's your birthday."

Later in the parlor, it was time for Gloria to open her gifts. She sat in the best chair in the room, a pretty rocking chair with flowered fabric.

"Open mine first, Glory." Harry handed her a paper rolled up like a scroll and tied with a pretty blue ribbon on each end.

"It looks too pretty to open, Harry. Did you wrap this by yourself?"

Larry was glad Gloria at least smiled at Harry.

Harry leaned against her knees. "Yes." He nodded once, hard.

Gloria and Larry both laughed. Larry was pretty sure Harry hadn't tied those ribbons all by himself. Mother had probably asked him to hold the paper while she tied the ribbons.

Harry said in a loud whisper, "After you open the present, you can use the ribbons in your hair."

"What a good idea. They'll go perfect with my favorite school dress." She untied them carefully and unrolled the scroll. On it were pencil drawings of five stick people.

"It's a nice picture, Harry."

"It's our fambly." Harry never could pronounce *family* the right way. It was a standing joke. All the Allertons had started calling themselves a *fambly*.

Larry's gift was next. It was wrapped with brown paper and tied with store string. "You probably don't want to wear the string in your hair."

Gloria laughed. She wasn't as careful unwrapping his gift. When the wrap was off, she gasped. "Oh, Larry! An *Anne of Green Gables* book of my very own! I love Anne! Mabel has two Anne books. We've read them and read them."

"I know. That's why I bought you this one." He was pleased she liked it so much, although he didn't understand why girls couldn't like sensible books like the ones about Tom Swift. Still, it was fun giving presents when people liked them.

He'd used the money Mother had given him for helping around the house to buy the gift. He still hadn't paid Jack back for the money he lent him for the movie.

Mother set a huge box on Gloria's lap. On the box was the name of one of the best stores in Minneapolis. Gloria pulled off the top of the box. "It's the coat I wanted!"

She set the box on the large footstool nearby. In a flash, she had the coat out and was trying it on.

"Does it fit?" Mother asked. She felt the shoulders. "Do you have enough room?"

"Yes, Mother."

"Looks like a soldier's coat," Larry said.

Gloria gave him a superior look. "It's supposed to look like that. It's called the military style. All the girls are wearing them. Hadn't you noticed?"

"No. I don't pay much attention to girls' clothes."

Gloria rolled her eyes. "Boys!"

The coat did look like a soldier's coat. It was made from khaki-colored army cloth. Even the buttons looked like military buttons. There were two patch pockets on top and two on the bottom. The pockets had flaps that closed over them like envelopes and fastened with buttons. There was even a belt for the coat, like soldiers had on their coats.

"I like it, Glory," Harry said.

"Thank you. At least I can always count on you, Harry."

Mother frowned. "Isn't there anything more in the box?"

Before Gloria could look, Harry was digging in the box. "A hat! A soldier's hat!" He pulled the khaki-colored hat over his hair as far as it would go. The hat wasn't very big, and it was almost diamond shaped.

Harry beamed, sending the rest of the Allertons into laughter.

"Good thing it really looks like a soldier's hat," Larry said, "because Harry might not let you have it back, Gloria."

At least Gloria is back to her usual nice self, he thought, watching her chuckle.

Not for long! When the gifts were put away, she flopped back down into the rocker and pouted. Mother played the piano and Larry and Harry sang with her, but they couldn't get Gloria to sing along.

"Let's make up our Christmas boxes for Greg and Mark," Mother suggested.

Gloria scowled. "It isn't even Thanksgiving yet."

"It takes a long time for boxes to make it across the ocean. If they aren't mailed by Thanksgiving, they may not reach the boys."

Larry snorted. "They aren't boys, Mother. They're men. They fought in a war, you know."

Mother sighed. "You're right. It's hard for me to realize people I knew as babies are soldiers now."

They all worked together packing the boxes. One box was for Jack's brother, Greg. The other box was for their cousin Mark. Even though the war was over, the newspapers said the soldiers in France wouldn't be back until next year, 1919.

Into each box they put hard candy, nuts, pencils, and socks.

"Hey!" Larry grabbed Harry's hand. "Quit snitching the candy. There won't be any left for Greg and Mark."

Harry didn't open his fist. "But it's pretty, and it tastes good."

"You can have one piece," Mother said, "but the rest goes in the boxes."

Harry stuffed the candy that was in his hand into his mouth. Larry was pretty sure there had been more than one piece in his little brother's hand, but he didn't say anything. Greg and Mark wouldn't want it now, anyway!

"Why don't you draw pictures for Greg and Mark, Harry?" Mother suggested. "Like you did for Gloria."

They finished the packing quickly once Harry was busy drawing.

"Jack's family is sending a wristwatch to Greg for Christmas," Larry said. "They bought him a special one. Jack's mom wanted to give him one because he'll wear it all the time. Every time he looks at it, he'll remember them."

Larry hardly knew any men who wore wristwatches before the war. Some used to carry pocket watches. The army said every soldier needed to wear a wristwatch, so now every man wanted one.

"Has Jack's family heard from Greg yet?" Mother asked.

"No." *Was he even alive?* Larry wondered.

"His letters have probably been delayed somewhere. Remember how they sometimes would not hear from him for months and then get ten letters at a time?"

Larry nodded. A spark of hope lit in his chest.

"Before we mail the boxes, let's each write a note to stick inside each box," Mother suggested.

Gloria hadn't smiled the whole time they packed the boxes. Now she said, "It seems like everyone in the whole world is gone. Greg and Mark are across the ocean. Father has the flu. I can't even see Mabel. Mabel and I always eat birthday cake together on our birthdays. I can't even show her my presents."

Larry sighed. Wouldn't she ever cheer up and stay that way?

Mother picked up the boxes and placed them on top of the piano, where Harry couldn't get into the candy. "Mabel will enjoy seeing your presents more when she's feeling better. If you finish reading the Anne of Green Gables book, maybe you can let Mabel read it when she's well again."

Gloria flopped back in the chair and crossed her arms. "It's not the same as seeing her."

"Why not write her a note telling her about the book?" Mother asked. "Then she can be looking forward to reading it when she's better. I can bring the note tomorrow when I bring them dinner. Maybe you'd like to help me carry lunch over tomorrow, since it's Saturday."

Mother had been making soup for Mabel's family ever since they saw the quarantine sign on their door. Everyone in Mabel's family had the flu. Every day Mother would take the soup and some fruit over and leave it on their porch, like the Boy Scouts had done with their soup deliveries.

But when Larry and Gloria went with their mother to take the soup the next day, they saw something that knocked everything out of their thoughts. On the door of Mabel's house was a black crepe bow.

Larry felt like someone had hit him in the stomach with a rock. He and Gloria stared at each other, their eyes huge. No one asked the question they were all thinking.

Who had died?

Chapter 6
The New Law

"Go home, children," Mother said quietly.

Larry swallowed the lump that filled his throat. "Can't we stay and find out who—"

"I'll speak with them. You two wait at home."

Larry took Gloria's hand. "Come on."

Gloria looked back over her shoulder at Mabel's house all the way to the street. Mother didn't go up to the door until Larry and Gloria had crossed the street and gone into their own home.

Without even taking off their coats and hats, Larry and Gloria hurried to the large front window where they could watch. They saw their mother knock on the door then move back to the sidewalk. The door opened, but only a little way. They couldn't tell who was talking to Mother.

It seemed all day before Mother turned around and came back home, but from the clock on the mantle, Larry knew it was only a few minutes.

They met her in the hall. She came inside, closed the door, and leaned back against it. Larry couldn't remember ever seeing her face so white.

"It's Violet," she said in a very quiet voice. "Violet is dead."

Larry dropped down onto the steps that led to the second floor. Violet! Pretty Violet, who had been so excited to train as a nurse and help sick soldiers alongside cousin Lydia. Violet, who had waited eagerly for Greg's letters from France.

Gloria slowly lowered herself to the bench in the hall. Her shoulders began to shake. She covered her face with her hands and began to sob.

That afternoon, Jack came over and asked Larry to go to the park with him. Larry didn't know what to say to Jack while they walked. Did Jack know about Violet? He didn't know how to talk about it.

Finally when they'd reached the park, Larry gathered up his courage and cleared his throat. "Did you hear? I mean, about. . .about Violet?"

Jack nodded, staring at his shoes scrunching through the fallen autumn leaves.

"It's. . .kind of rough for Greg, I guess," Larry added.

Was that the wrong thing to say? he wondered.

"Maybe." Jack pressed his lips together hard for a minute. "Maybe he'll never know. Maybe he's dead, too. Maybe he'll never come back."

The pain in his friend's voice made Larry's chest hurt. He wished he could say something that would help. He didn't want to lie to him, though. Greg was a soldier. They both knew he could be dead.

"Maybe that's true," Larry said slowly. "Or maybe his letters were lost somewhere."

Jack snorted.

"Well, they could be. Maybe they were on a ship that was sunk or something."

Jack darted him a sharp glance. "I guess maybe that could have happened. Those old Germans sank a lot of our boats."

Was that a little bit of hope he heard in Jack's voice?

Jack pulled out his slingshot. "Bring your new sling?"

"Yes." Larry took it out of his pocket. He thrilled at the smooth feel of it. He remembered the times Jack had let him try his slingshot. "Want to try it?"

Jack shook his head. "Maybe later." He grinned his one-sided grin. "After you break it in."

Larry and Jack practiced on twigs and leaves and a couple empty glass bottles they found. Then Jack started aiming at birds.

At first, Larry only watched him. Then he heard a "chirp chirp." Looking about, he spotted a cardinal in a nearby tree. A wave of excitement surged through him. He took careful aim and pulled back the sling. A pebble flew through the air. A moment later, the red bird lay on the ground.

He walked over and nudged it with the toe of his shoe. The bird was dead.

Goosebumps spread over his arms. He felt sick to his stomach. A minute ago, the cardinal had been talking to him from the branch. Now it would never chirp again. All because of him. He had the power to take life away from something.

Suddenly, anger rolled through him. "Sissy!" he said under his breath. "It's only a dumb old bird."

From the corner of his eye, he saw a movement. A gray squirrel was running across the leaf-covered ground. It jumped onto the trunk of a tree, looked at Larry for a moment, then raced up the tree to sit on a branch and chatter at him.

Larry looked for another stone. Aimed. *Whiz!*

"Missed! I'll get you next time."

The squirrel didn't wait for next time. He darted away.

It took a few more tries before Larry hit another bird. This time when he looked at the lifeless fellow, he didn't feel sorry for it a bit. Instead it felt good to know he was getting good enough with the slingshot to be able to hit things like Jack could.

After all, he reminded himself, *like Jack said, men in the war killed each other. What did it matter if a few birds died?*

He couldn't keep Greg and Mark away from the danger of war, and he couldn't keep people from getting the flu and dying of it, but he could shoot things with a slingshot. Why should only people have to die?

"There's a new city law," Miss Wilson told the class Monday morning. "Boys are no longer allowed to carry slingshots in the city."

"What?" Larry jerked up straight in his seat.

Groans and questions from boys in the room filled the air. "Why?"

"They can't do that!"

"They're always trying to keep us from doing things that are fun!"

Miss Wilson held up her hands. "Boys, please!" When they'd quieted down, she said, "There is a reason for the new law. Boys have been using BB guns and slingshots for vandalism. They've shot out street lights, and policemen say boys have killed hundreds of birds in the parks while school was closed for the flu."

"Aw, man!"

"They're only birds!"

"That's not fair!"

Miss Wilson rapped the wooden yardstick she used as a pointer on her desk. "Boys! Boys!" The uproar died down to a grumbling rumble. "I'm sorry, but the law is the law. If anyone is seen with a slingshot on school grounds, I or another teacher will take it away. If policemen see you with slingshots, the police will take them away."

Larry raised his hand. "Even if we aren't shooting birds or anything?"

Miss Wilson nodded. "Even if you aren't shooting anything."

Larry raised his hand again. "How can they make laws kids have to obey when kids don't get to vote?"

"Yes!" others called out. "What about that?"

Miss Wilson laughed. "There are a lot of people who don't get to vote for the lawmakers and have to follow the laws anyway. Visitors from other countries have to follow our laws. Women have to follow the laws. Neither visitors nor most women have the right to vote. There are soldiers who fought in the Great War who weren't old enough to vote when they went into the service to die for their country."

Larry crossed his arms over his chest and slid down in his chair. He didn't like her answer, but he didn't have a good argument against it. "Well, it isn't fair."

"When you grow up, Larry, you can ask the men you vote for to make laws you think *are* fair."

When he grew up and could vote? That seemed a long way away. Like forever.

Larry was still angry when he got home.

Mother had baked, and the kitchen was still warm and smelled like fresh cookies. She'd placed a few on a plate on the kitchen table and poured glasses of cold milk for Larry, Gloria, and Harry. While they ate, Larry told Mother of the new law.

"I think it's a good law." Gloria reached for another cookie. "I think it's mean to kill birds."

Larry snorted.

"Besides," Gloria said, "sometimes mean boys used their slingshots to shoot stones at girls in the schoolyard or after school on their way home."

"You never told me that." Mother frowned.

Gloria shrugged. "Boys are always doing mean things."

"Not all boys," Larry defended.

"No, but the bullies do."

Larry took another bite of his cookie. He was so angry that it didn't even taste good.

Mother had a strange, sad look on her face. She hadn't said anything more about the boys who shot at the girls with their slingshots. *Is something wrong?* Larry wondered.

Suddenly he remembered that he hadn't asked about Father when he got home from school. "Did you see Father today?"

"He's still in bed." She took a long, shaky breath. "I have some news but not about Father."

Larry lowered his cookie slowly to the table, watching his mother's face all the time. A strange feeling went through him. He didn't think he wanted to hear Mother's news.

"What is it, Mother?" Gloria asked.

Mother took another shaky breath. "It's Mabel's little brother, Charlie. He died of the flu this morning."

CHAPTER 7
A Special Thanksgiving

Charlie, dead!

Larry stared at Mother in disbelief. Charlie was the same age as Harry. He could remember when they had been babies. He'd seen him grow up—all the way to five years old. Charlie couldn't be dead.

Gloria dropped her head into her hands and began sobbing. Mother put her arms around her, but Gloria kept crying.

Harry started crying, too. Larry didn't think Harry understood that he'd never see his little friend again, but Harry knew something was awfully wrong.

Larry jumped up, bolted down the hall, grabbed his coat and hat, and slammed the door behind him.

He didn't know where he was going, but he had to go somewhere. He had to do something. He couldn't bear to just sit around and feel hurt and sad and angry.

He ran down the sidewalk, not looking at Mabel's house with the two black ribbons on the door. He ran and ran until he came to the park. In the middle of the park, he threw himself down on the cold ground in the middle of musty autumn leaves beside a thicket of bare lilac bushes. He didn't think anyone could see him.

Tears burned his eyes. He buried his head in his arms and sobbed. "It's crazy! The whole world's gone crazy! Stupid war! Stupid Old Spanish Lady flu!"

When he couldn't cry anymore, he stood up and brushed the leaves off his coat and wool trousers. A flicker sang from one of the top branches of the lilac bush. Anger flooded him. Why should a bird have life so easy when his life was so hard? He tugged his slingshot from his pocket and found a pebble in the leaf-covered grass.

Whiz!

The song ended.

Thanksgiving morning, Larry woke up sad. It seemed to him he'd awakened sad every day since hearing about Charlie. The smell of roasting turkey finally lured him from his bed. Mother had said she was going to get up at four to begin making Thanksgiving dinner.

At least they would have company for Thanksgiving. Grandma Allerton, Aunt Esther and Uncle Erik, and their five-year-old daughter, Adeline, were coming for dinner.

"I suppose that's one thing to be thankful for," he mumbled, tucking his shirttail into his trousers as he stumbled downstairs.

Gloria was just going downstairs, too. She raised her arms above her head and yawned widely. Gloria always woke up slowly.

"Morning," they said to each other.

Because it was Thanksgiving and they were having company, Gloria was wearing her favorite dress. It was white with ruffles trimmed in pale blue. She carried the blue ribbons Harry had given her for her birthday. They matched the edges of the ruffles.

Together they walked into the kitchen.

"Hi, Larry and Gloria. Happy Thanksgiving!"

Larry stopped cold and stared. "Father!"

"Father!" Gloria echoed.

Father grinned at them. He sat in a straight-backed white wooden chair at one end of the kitchen table.

Gloria dashed across the room, her best black shoes clattering on the linoleum. She threw her arms around Father's neck. "You're home! I *missed* you!"

"I missed you, too, sweetheart. I missed all of you."

Larry was right behind Gloria. He would have given Father a hug, too, but Gloria wouldn't let go of Father's neck. Father reached out a hand to grasp one of Larry's. Larry held it tight. Surprise flickered through him at the weakness of Father's grip.

"Hello, Son."

"No one told us you were coming home," Larry accused. "When did you get here?"

"About an hour ago. Uncle Erik picked me up and brought me home."

Mother came over, wiping her hands on the large apron that covered all of her dress except her sleeves. She was smiling the biggest smile Larry had seen on her face in weeks. "Father and I were hoping he would be home today, but I didn't tell you because I didn't want you to be disappointed if he couldn't make it."

Gloria loosened her hold on Father's neck enough to look in his face. "But you're well, now, aren't you? You're over that mean old flu!"

Father nodded, smiling.

Mother cautioned, "Father's doctor says Father still needs lots of rest. So I want you children to be careful not to tire him out too much. Promise?"

Gloria and Larry promised.

While Mother worked on Thanksgiving dinner, Gloria and Larry brought Father up to date on family and school life. Gloria showed him all her birthday presents.

Finally Gloria leaned against Father's knees and said in a low voice, "Violet and Charlie died from the flu."

"Yes. Mother told me. We'll miss them, won't we?"

Gloria's pointed chin lifted, and her blue eyes flashed with anger and tears. "If you hadn't been sick, you would have helped them, wouldn't you? Then they wouldn't have died."

Father rested a large hand on her cheek. "I would have done everything I could to make them well. But I can't save everyone I help, sweetheart. No doctor is able to do that. This flu is very dangerous. Every doctor is losing lots of flu patients."

"But I wanted Violet and Charlie to get better!" A tear rolled over her cheek and dripped onto one of her blue-edged ruffles.

"I know. Mother and I wanted them to get better, too. They

were special people. Weren't we lucky to know them?"

Gloria nodded, wiping the tear away with the back of her hand.

Larry thought they were lucky to have known Violet and Charlie, too. He knew they would see them again in heaven, but he wished they could have spent more time on earth!

When Harry woke up and discovered Father was home, he climbed into Father's lap and stayed there. He patted his Father's sunken cheeks with both hands. "Poor Papa was sick. Now Papa is all better."

Soon the Moes and Grandma Allerton arrived. They surrounded Father in the hot kitchen with welcomes and questions. Finally Mother shooed them into the parlor so she had room to work.

Harry tugged at Grandma Allerton's skirt. "Where's Grandpa?"

"Grandpa is with the army now, remember? He left last month."

"Oh. I forgot." Harry's eyebrows met in a frown. Larry was pretty sure Harry didn't remember Grandpa leaving at all!

Larry had been surprised when Grandpa left to work at the army camp hospital. It seemed funny to think of an old man like Grandpa working in the army! He wasn't exactly a soldier. When the war started, Grandpa had joined the Volunteer Medical Service Corps like thousands of other retired doctors. These doctors promised to help if needed because so many younger doctors were in the army.

In September, lots of soldiers at training camps in the United States started dying from the Spanish flu. That's when doctors like Grandpa in the Volunteer Corps were sent to the camps to help.

"It seems strange to have Thanksgiving without Grandpa here," Larry said to Grandma.

It felt strange without Aunt Anna and Uncle Hans's family, too. All of Lydia's family caught the flu after Lydia came down with it. *At least none of them died,* Larry thought. They were all over the flu now, but too weak to be visiting.

Gloria helped set the dining room table for the big dinner. She liked using the lace tablecloth and Mother's best china and crystal. The table looked so pretty when it was set, with the sunshine through the lace curtains making the crystal glitter.

When Mother announced dinner was ready, everyone hurried to the dining room and stood behind their chairs. Uncle Erik read an article from the newspaper written by President Woodrow Wilson. It was called the Thanksgiving Proclamation. Uncle Erik said the president sent the article to all the major newspapers in the country.

"It has long been our custom," Uncle Erik read, "to turn in the autumn of the year in praise and thanksgiving to Almighty God for His many blessings and mercies to us as a nation. This year we have special and moving cause to be grateful and to rejoice. God has in His good pleasure given us peace. It has come as a great triumph of right. Complete victory has brought us, not peace alone, but the confident promise of a new day as well, in which justice shall replace force and jealousy between nations.

"God has indeed been gracious. We have cause for such rejoicing as revives and strengthens in us all the best traditions of our national history. A new day shines about us, in which our hearts take new courage and look forward with new hope to new and greater duties.

"While we render thanks for these things, let us not forget

to seek the divine guidance in the performance of those duties, and divine mercy and forgiveness for all errors of act or purpose, and pray that in all that we do we shall strengthen the ties of friendship and mutual respect upon which we build the new structure of peace and good will among the nations.

"Wherefore, I, Woodrow Wilson, President of the United States of America, do hereby designate Thursday, the twenty-eighth day of November, as a day of thanksgiving and prayer, and invite the people throughout the land to cease upon that day from their ordinary occupations and in their several homes and places of worship to render thanks to God, the ruler of nations."

When Erik finished, Father said grace. Then everyone sat down to enjoy the big, wonderful-smelling meal in front of them.

After dinner, Larry and Gloria sat together on the bottom step in the hallway. Larry took a deep breath. "Turkey, dressing, mashed potatoes and gravy, cranberries, and lots of pumpkin pie for dessert. I'm stuffed!"

Gloria leaned back against the steps. "Me, too."

Through the etched glass window in the front door, Larry could see Harry and five-year-old Adeline playing. Adeline was seated in the little red wooden wagon that had been a Christmas present to Larry a few years earlier. Harry was pulling her about the leaf-covered yard, pretending he was a horse.

Harry threw back his head and went "Neigh! Neigh!" then stomped his foot like a horse stomping his hoof.

"Giddap!" Adeline called, holding on to the high wagon sides.

Larry laughed. "Remember when I used to pull you in the wagon that way, Glory?"

"You made a good horse." She giggled.

"Boy, thanks a lot!"

Grandma Allerton and Aunt Esther were helping Mother clean up the dishes. Father and Uncle Erik were visiting in the parlor, where Father could rest in a comfortable chair while they talked.

Gloria whispered, "Father doesn't look very good, does he? His coat is almost too big for him. There are gray circles beneath his eyes, and his face is skinnier than before. When Harry asked him to play catch with him, he told Harry he felt too tired to play."

A frown wrinkled her brow. "Father never used to be too tired to play with us a *little* bit, anyway."

"No. I guess he's tired from having the flu." Her words made Larry uneasy. He'd noticed the changes in Father, too.

"Do you think he is really over the flu? Maybe he looks so bad because he is still sick."

Larry shook his head. "No. He wouldn't have come home if he still had the flu. Remember how worried he always is about people spreading the flu to other people? He wouldn't have come home if he thought he might give us the flu."

"I suppose not." Gloria's eyes still looked troubled. "I'm glad he's home, but I wish he was like he used to be."

"He will be. By Christmas, he'll be his old self."

"You think so?"

"Sure." Larry wasn't sure at all, but he wanted Gloria to feel better. Besides, he wanted Father back to his old self, too.

Larry and Gloria could hear Father and Uncle Erik's voices through the double doors of the parlor that were open to the hallway.

"This flu is as much a war for doctors as the Great War was

a war for soldiers," Uncle Erik was saying.

"Yes, and a horrible war. We can't simply agree to sign a peace treaty for the war on flu," Father answered.

Larry leaned forward and breathed quietly. Even Father's voice sounded tired. He saw that Gloria was listening to the men, too.

"How are things at City Hospital?" Erik asked.

"Bad. Other doctors are sick. Half the nurses are sick and have been for weeks. We've asked the Great Lakes Naval Training Center to send sailors to work as nurses at the hospital."

"Sailors? Are they trained as nurses?"

"No. But they've been through the flu, so we don't need to worry they will catch it from the patients. Also, sailors know how to take orders. We can teach them how to help with the patients. If they send the sailors, we can open up three more wards for flu patients at the hospital. Right now we have to turn away ambulances that bring patients. We've no place to put them."

Larry's stomach tightened. He couldn't imagine a hospital sending patients away! Where would they go?

"Have any of the new vaccines been tried at City Hospital?" Uncle Erik asked.

"No. A lot of doctors are trying to find vaccines and cures, but nothing's worked yet. The doctors at the Mayo Clinic are working on a vaccine, and I'd hoped to get some. I wired a friend who is a doctor there. He wired back that although early tests of the vaccine showed it might work sometimes, it hadn't been proven to prevent the flu. There wasn't enough serum to send us even if it did work. Mayo has been swamped with letters and wires from all over the world asking for help."

"Do you think there's a chance someone will come up with

a new medicine to cure the flu?" Uncle Erik was asking Father all kind of questions, just like he was interviewing him for the newspaper.

"I wish! In the last hundred years or so, we've found ways to prevent or cure all kinds of diseases that used to kill thousands of people: smallpox, typhoid, malaria, yellow fever, cholera, diphtheria. But we haven't found a way to stop or cure the flu."

"At least it hasn't been as bad here as in some other places," Uncle Erik said. "In Spruce Creek, Alaska, the flu wiped out the entire village."

Larry and Gloria stared at each other.

"The whole village!" Father exclaimed. "I hadn't heard about that. I suppose the natives hadn't been exposed to as much flu through the years as most people in the United States. What a shame!"

"Boston, Philadelphia, New York—I hear they've all been hit hard. In New York City, 851 people died in one day! In Philadelphia, over 11,000 people have died so far," Uncle Erik reported. "They don't even have enough coffins. Some people have stolen coffins. The dead are put in wooden boxes on their front porches, and trucks drive by and pick them up. Sometimes dead bodies lay in the gutters."

"We learned from the eastern cities' mistakes," Father said. "The flu started in the army camps. Healthy young men came down with the flu and died by the thousands after being sick only a couple days. They spread it to the cities near the camps. The cities' health officers didn't know at first how easily this flu spreads—or how quickly. When they realized this flu was killing their people, they closed the schools, entertainment centers, and churches.

"Our city learned from them. We didn't wait until many people died before closing places where people were apt to spread the flu to each other."

"How many have died of the flu here?" Uncle Erik asked.

"We don't know for sure." Father snorted. "About seven hundred have been reported in Minneapolis and the same in St. Paul. So far."

"So far," Uncle Erik repeated.

The words sent chills down Larry's spine. More people would die before it was over.

"Did you hear that the editor of the St. Paul newspaper, the *Pioneer Press,* died?" Uncle Erik asked. "His wife died a few days before he did. They left two children, orphans now."

"Too many of them." Father's voice was sad.

"Senator Albert Fall lost two children to the flu, but he survived it," Uncle Erik added. "You never know who the Spanish Lady will take."

"I'm worried about Frances."

Father's words caught Larry by surprise. Why would he be worried about Mother?

"She's going to have a baby, Erik, the end of May."

Gloria gasped and clapped a hand over her mouth.

Larry's mouth dropped open. He and Gloria stared at each other. A baby!

CHAPTER 8
Mabel's Story

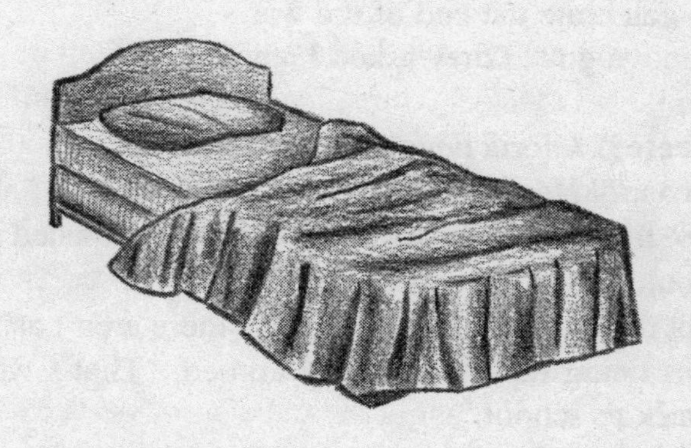

It was the first time Larry and Gloria had heard about the baby. Adults didn't tell children about babies until the babies were born. It wasn't considered proper. Even hearing Father tell Uncle Erik about it made Larry's cheeks hot with embarrassment. But it was fun, too, to think about a new baby coming to live in their house.

Larry walked softly over to stand by the open parlor doors so he could hear the men better. Gloria followed.

"If Frances catches the flu," Father was saying to Erik, "it could be very dangerous for her. Pregnant women have a greater chance of dying if they catch the flu than most other people. Even if they don't die, many of them lose their unborn babies."

Larry bit his bottom lip and looked at Gloria. He could see fear in her blue eyes. He knew she could see it in his eyes, too. Fear was tying his stomach into a tight, painful knot.

After a supper made up of leftovers from the big Thanksgiving dinner, Uncle Erik got ready to go to the Victory Sing. He had to go so he could write an article on it for the newspaper. Thousands of people were expected to go to the Victory Sing to celebrate the end of the war.

"Can we go?" Larry asked Father.

"No."

"Please?" Gloria begged.

"Please?" Harry asked.

"No. It's too dangerous to go to such a crowded place. The city should never have allowed it."

"But the city health director says there aren't as many new flu cases being reported," Larry argued. "That's why we had to go back to school."

Father just shook his head. "This Victory Sing will only bring more people together and spread the flu faster. In a few days, we'll see more flu cases because of the Victory Sing. Mark my words."

Larry crossed his arms and plopped down in a wooden rocker with a leather seat.

"I have an idea." Grandma Allerton clapped her hands together. "Let's have our own Victory Sing. The songs they were going to sing are listed in the paper. We can sing the same ones."

Grandma sat down on the round piano stool, and everyone stood about her. Father leaned against the side of the tall piano.

While Grandma played, they sang some of their favorite songs: "America," "Battle Hymn of the Republic," "America the Beautiful," "There's a Long, Long Trail A-windin'," "Keep the Home Fires Burning," and "When Johnny Comes Marching Home."

One of their favorites was "Pack Up Your Troubles in Your Old Kit Bag and Smile, Smile, Smile." Larry, Gloria, Harry, and Adeline sang as loud as they could on that one and tried to smile at the same time. By the end of the song they were laughing too hard at each other to sing.

The last song was "Praise God From Whom All Blessings Flow," to thank God for bringing victory in the war and peace to America and the other countries.

While they sang, Larry looked out across the street. He could see a light in one of the upstairs bedroom windows at Mabel's house. He didn't think they would be celebrating at Mabel's tonight.

He didn't feel like laughing anymore. He felt sad.

Everyone knew the men who went to war might not come back, but no one expected so many of their neighbors and relatives to get sick and die. *Why is it happening, God?* he asked silently. *If You can stop a world war, why won't You stop the Old Spanish Lady?*

"Larry! Larry! Did you hear? Did you hear the news?"

Larry stuck his head out his bedroom door at the sound of Jack's voice. His friend was bounding up the last of the stairs, a huge smile on his face.

Larry spread his arms. "I just left you at your house fifteen minutes ago when we got home from school. What could have happened in fifteen minutes?"

"Haven't you read the newspaper? The first American troops from Europe arrived in New York Harbor yesterday!"

Larry's heart seemed to jump to attention. It beat as fast as if he'd run a mile. "The 151st, the Gopher Gunners, Greg's regiment?"

"Nope." Jack's smile grew smaller, but his face was still filled with more hope than Larry had seen there in months. "The article says the 151st won't be back from France until next year."

"Next year isn't so far away," Larry tried to cheer his friend. "It's already the second of December."

"Yeah." Jack's smile widened again. "At least the first troops have started coming home, not just soldiers who were hurt in the war."

Many badly injured soldiers had already returned to the States. Lydia was helping with some of them at the hospital at Fort Snelling on the Mississippi River in St. Paul.

Larry was glad Father was home for dinner that night. Even though he was recovering from the flu and needed a lot of rest, he was still helping at the hospital. He'd worked both Saturday and Sunday, coming home after Larry, Gloria, and Harry were in bed.

"Why can you come home now?" Gloria asked. "Before you were afraid you might bring us the flu."

"Now that I've had the flu, I'm immune."

Gloria looked puzzled. "What does that mean?"

"It means I can't catch that kind of flu again. My body can fight it off."

"Good!" Gloria heaved a sigh of relief.

"Good!" Harry copied her sigh, causing the family to burst out with laughter.

It feels so good to be together like a real family again, Larry thought. Pleasure filled his chest with warmth.

"Jack and I saw a great flicker Saturday, Father," Larry said. "It's the new Charlie Chaplin show, *Shoulder Arms*." He laughed just remembering it. "Charlie was a rookie soldier, and—"

"What side was he fighting for?" Gloria asked.

"Our side, of course! He was a Yank. Anyway, he captured old Kaiser Bill single-handed and the crown prince, von Hindenburg, too!"

Father smiled. "Sounds like we could have used him in the real war. But I didn't know you were going to the theater. I don't want you to go again unless I say you might."

Anger seemed to roll up from Larry's toes and fill him. "A fellow can't do anything fun anymore because of that old flu! The city wouldn't have opened the theaters again if they weren't safe, would they?"

"Larry!"

Mother's shocked protest reminded him he'd spoken out of turn. Father's face was red with surprise and anger. He and Mother were fair, but they didn't allow their children to speak disrespectfully to them. Larry knew he should apologize, but he was so mad!

"What did you say?" his father asked quietly.

There was anger beneath Father's quiet voice. Larry swallowed hard. His chest rose and fell in angry breaths. "I'm sorry, but I'm still mad we can't do anything fun because of the flu."

Father set his fork down and looked Larry in the eye. "I don't agree with some of the city officials that it's all right to open schools and theaters again and let people gather for things like the Victory Sing. Only two days after the sing, 450 new cases of flu were reported. That means the flu is on the upswing again."

Larry bit his bottom lip. He didn't want Father to be right.

"Everyone is tired of the flu epidemic," Father said. "People will listen to any promise because they want to believe they can't catch it. The newspapers are full of ads for remedies that won't help prevent or cure it, but people buy them anyway. Things like Miller's Snake Oil and Dr. Pierce's Pleasant Pellets and Koynos Dental Cream and Horlick's Malted Milk. The only thing that will keep the flu away is staying away from people who might have it. Understand?"

"Yes, Father," Larry mumbled, staring at his plate.

He'd been around people ever since the flu started. Couldn't help it! He'd been at school, he'd played with Jack and their friends, and he'd helped with Boy Scout projects. Wouldn't he have caught the flu by now if he was going to catch it? Maybe he was immune like Father was now.

The next day, Mabel came to school with them for the first time since she came down with the flu. She looked almost as bad as Father. Her dress and coat hung loose. She looked very tired.

After lunch, Gloria, Mabel, Larry, and Jack went outdoors with most of the rest of the school for a short break before afternoon classes began. Children were playing in groups all over the schoolyard: dodgeball, catch, footraces, marbles, jump rope.

Larry, Jack, and Gloria stood near the door of the building at the top of the stone steps, staying out of the wind and listening to Mabel tell about the weeks she and her family had the flu. Her parents and thirteen-year-old sister, Opal, had survived, but they missed Violet and Charlie.

"It was awful," Mabel said in a low, sad voice. "Everyone in the family was sick. We took turns helping each other. The one who felt the best would help. Then when someone else was stronger, they would help. Sometimes, no one was strong enough to get out of bed."

"Did you have to take care of your father and mother?" Gloria's voice sounded like she couldn't imagine such a thing. Larry couldn't, either.

Mabel nodded. "Some days I had to take care of everyone."

"What did you do for them?" Glory asked.

"There wasn't much I could do. I heated the soup your mother brought and gave that to them. I had to feed them with a spoon sometimes, because they were so weak. And I gave them water or pieces of the oranges your mother brought when they were thirsty."

"Wow! That sounds tough, Mabel," Jack said.

Gloria placed an arm around Mabel's shoulders. "I missed you, Mabel. I'm glad you're feeling better and are back at school with us."

Larry and Jack nodded.

Larry watched Mabel's gaze search the school grounds where kids were laughing and playing. "It doesn't seem very important to come to school anymore," she said. "Nothing seems important anymore. How can everything stay the same when Violet and Charlie are dead?"

Gloria's troubled eyes met Larry's. "We miss Violet and Charlie, too. We're sorry, Mabel."

"Yes," Larry agreed.

Jack nodded.

Three girls skipping rope at the bottom of the steps began chanting:

"I had a little bird
It's name was Enza.
I opened up the window
And in-flew-Enza."

Mabel burst into tears and tore down the steps.

"Mabel!" Gloria called as she and Larry and Jack watched her run across the schoolyard.

Mabel kept running.

Gloria started down the steps after her. Before she reached the bottom, the school bell rang to tell the students it was time to come inside.

"Better come inside," Larry told her. "I think Mabel is going home."

Gloria slowly climbed back up the steps, watching Mabel over her shoulder. "Do you think she'll be okay?"

"I don't know." No one in Larry and Gloria's family had died, not since they were born. It felt awful having friends like Violet and Charlie die. What must it be like to lose your sister and brother? "I don't know if she'll be okay."

Chapter 9

A New Project

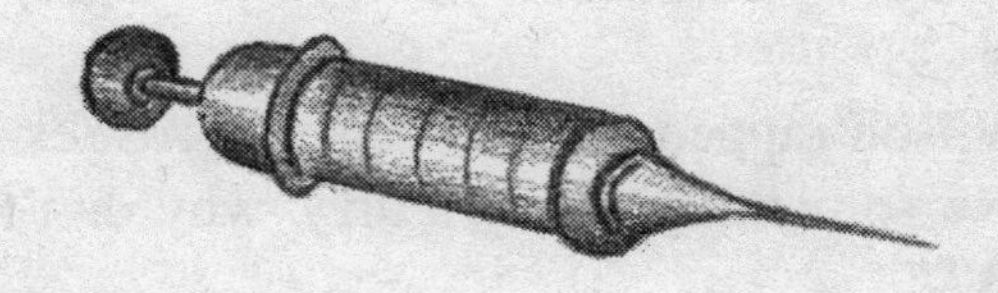

That afternoon was one of the strangest in Larry's life.

Classes started as usual after the noon break. In arithmetic, they were learning about triangles. Larry thought it was interesting. How exciting, he thought, to be able to determine so many things about the size of a triangle from only pieces of information!

Suddenly Miss Wilson turned from the blackboard and slammed the yardstick she'd been using as a pointer against her desk. "Albert Moss, wake up!"

Larry jumped in surprise. He looked at the desk next to his. He'd been listening so hard to Miss Wilson that he hadn't noticed Al lay his head down on his arms. He and Al were pretty good friends. They were in the same Boy Scout troop.

Now Al was blinking like he'd just awakened.

"See if you can stay awake for the rest of the afternoon, Mr. Moss." Miss Wilson turned back to the blackboard amidst the giggles of the class.

Al's cheeks were red. Larry grinned. No wonder his friend was embarrassed!

Larry leaned across the aisle and whispered, "Want me to sing you a lullaby?"

Al neither laughed nor shot him a dirty look. His head rolled a bit like he really was trying to keep from falling asleep.

"Hey, what's the matter with you?" Larry asked, still whispering.

Miss Wilson rapped the end of her yardstick on the floor. "If you have something to say, Larry, why don't you tell the whole class?"

Larry pressed his lips together hard. Why did teachers always say things like that? Hadn't any teacher anywhere ever had to say anything to a friend that couldn't wait until class was over?

Much to Larry's relief, she turned her attention back to Al. "Albert, why don't you stand up and tell the class the formula to determine the hypotenuse of the triangle?"

Al stared at her but didn't stand or say anything.

Didn't he hear her? Larry wondered. "Al, stand up!" he whispered. *Maybe he can't remember the formula.* But Miss Wilson had just told them the formula a few minutes ago.

Al slowly pushed himself to his feet. His face was screwed into pain. With one hand he rubbed the top of his leg. With the other, he leaned on his desk. Larry could hear him panting.

Miss Wilson took a couple steps toward him. A worried frown cut between her eyebrows. "Are you all right?"

Al shut his eyes. Opened them again. "My legs hurt. They hurt real bad."

Miss Wilson hurried down the aisle. Before she reached Al's desk, Al slumped to the floor.

"Al!" Larry jumped to his feet. Fear caught at his throat. What was happening to his friend?

"You should have seen him, Father," Larry said at dinner that night. "Al was fine at lunchtime. He was playing dodgeball. An hour later, he couldn't stand up! The nurse told Miss Wilson Al has the flu. Could the flu do that to a guy?"

Father's lips pressed hard together and he nodded. "The Spanish flu can do that and worse. It killed many strong young men in the army in only two days."

"Some students in my class got sick today, too," Gloria said, "but no one was so sick they couldn't stand up."

Larry nodded. "I saw other kids get sick and have to go home today, too."

Father crumpled up his napkin and threw it down beside his plate. "That's it. You two aren't going back to school until this epidemic is over."

Harry stared at him over the piece of bread he was eating. Larry didn't wonder Harry stared. He'd seldom heard his father's voice so angry.

"We have to go to school, Father," Gloria said.

Larry nodded. "Don't we?"

"I'm not goin' to school," Harry piped up.

Father had already told Mother to keep Harry home from school, but Harry was only five. He wasn't learning important things like how to figure out how long the side of a triangle is!

Father ignored Harry. "You're not going back, Larry and

Glory. That's final. The city health director told the school officials this would happen if they opened the schools again, but they wouldn't listen!"

"The principal told us at a school meeting that there weren't many students our age catching the flu," Larry said. "He said that babies and older people were catching it, mostly. No one our age has died from it."

"Not in Minneapolis," Father agreed. "Not yet. In October and November, not many children your age came down with the flu. Some did, like Mabel."

Larry and Gloria nodded.

"In the last week," Father continued, "half the new cases of flu are among schoolchildren. I'm glad children your age haven't been dying of the flu. But that doesn't mean they can't spread it to other people in their families."

"You mean we could catch the flu, and then Mother and Harry could catch it from us?" Larry asked.

"Yes." Father's shoulders relaxed a bit. "I'm sorry, you two. I know you'll miss seeing your friends, but it's not safe to go back to school."

They had no other choice but to do as he said.

Later, when Larry and Gloria were in the parlor with Father alone, he told them why he was so worried. "The Spanish flu is most dangerous for children Harry's age and younger and for people fifteen to thirty-five." He took a deep breath. "Mother is going to have a baby, so her body can't fight off the flu very well. It's very important we try to keep Mother and Harry from catching the flu."

Larry and Gloria nodded. Neither one told him they already knew about the baby!

"It's so important that Mother and Harry don't get sick,"

Father continued, "that I'm going to vaccinate all of you tonight."

Larry looked at him in surprise. "I thought you said there wasn't a vaccine against the flu that works."

"This isn't against the flu. It's against pneumonia. The flu attacks the lungs. If it hurts the lungs badly enough, the person gets pneumonia. It's the pneumonia the flu causes that usually kills people."

Gloria nodded, the red bow of the ribbon tied about her hair bouncing. "But this shot you give us will keep us from catching new. . .new. . ."

"Pneumonia," Larry finished.

Father sighed. "I don't know whether the shot will stop it or not. There's never been a vaccine for pneumonia before. People at the University of Minnesota just came up with it. Most of the professors at the university and their families are being vaccinated with it. It's worth a try."

Larry and Gloria weren't so sure they wanted to try it when Father brought out the needle, but they held their breaths and rolled up their sleeves for the shot anyway.

Larry thought the next morning would never end. Life had seemed boring enough when school was closed. Now, they were the only ones at home. All their friends were still in school.

"I finally got to see Mabel again," Gloria complained as they stared out the front window together, "and now she's in school and I'm at home. I even gave her my new Anne of Green Gables book yesterday, so I can't read it again now."

Harry tugged at Larry's shirt sleeve. "Will you play army with me?"

Larry sighed. "Sure. Nothing else to do." Besides, Mother

had told him and Gloria they were to help her watch Harry while they were out of school.

Larry and Gloria were glad when Lydia came to dinner that evening. Someone new to talk to! She told them about the work she was doing for the wounded soldiers, or disabled veterans as she called them, at Fort Snelling.

"There are about five hundred of them," she said. "They've paid a high price for the victory we won in the war. Some have lost a hand, or an arm, or a leg—or both hands, arms, or legs. Some are blind or deaf. Some suffered from trench fever. It's sad to see what they've lost, but most still have their fighting spirits."

Father nodded. "I remember early in the war, when the Canadians had been fighting longer than America. The Canadians had already seen trainloads of their wounded soldiers return from battle, sometimes thousands at a time. The Canadians told the Americans when we entered the fight, 'Wait until your wounded begin to return. Only then will you realize what war really is.' "

Lydia nodded. "Yes, it is like that for me."

Larry wondered whether Jack's brother, Greg, would come back as one of the disabled veterans. *Maybe he won't come back at all.*

Lydia raised her eyebrows and looked around the dinner table with a smile and a question in her pretty eyes. "I was hoping you Allerton cousins could make some things for the disabled veterans. Christmas is coming up, and they can use some things."

"Sure!" Gloria sat up straight in her chair, her eyes gleaming. She always liked to make things and help out. She did things like that for Mother's suffrage group a lot.

"Can I help, too?" Harry asked.

"Especially you!" Lydia winked at him. He rewarded her with a grin.

"What do you want us to make?" Larry asked. He wasn't sure he really wanted to help, but at least it would be something to do until they could go back to school again.

"The vets need cloth bags."

"I can sew them," Gloria offered eagerly. "Maybe Larry and Harry can cut out the material for me."

"What do they do with the bags?" Larry asked.

"They keep small belongings in them," Lydia explained, "and hang them on their beds where they can reach them easily."

Harry climbed onto his knees and leaned on the table. "What can I make?"

Lydia smiled at him. "You can help Gloria and Larry make storybooks."

Disappointment sagged at Harry's shoulders. "I don't know how to do that."

"It's easy. You cut a short story out of a magazine and paste it into a homemade scrapbook. Paste some cartoons and jokes in, too. It gives the vets something to do. It's a bit boring for them at the hospital sometimes."

"What do they do there?" Gloria asked.

"Well, they have to rest a lot, of course. Some of them are trying to learn to walk with artificial legs or to use a wheelchair. One man who went deaf from having a shell explode too near him is learning to read lips. For entertainment, they read books, listen to phonograph records, or watch motion pictures."

Larry looked at her in surprise. "They have a theater at the hospital?"

Lydia laughed. "Nothing so fancy as that. The flickers are

shown on the ceiling. It's big and white, and patients who are lying on their backs can see it just fine."

Larry grinned at the thought of watching a movie from bed!

"Are the veterans from this part of the country?" Mother asked.

"They are from all over the United States. They used to do all kinds of things before they became soldiers. Some were farmers, some were factory workers, some were reporters. Remember Uncle Erik telling us about one hundred men from the Minneapolis *Tribune* being in the service? I met an especially nice veteran a few days ago. He's an engineer. His name is Donald Harrington."

Father gave Lydia a teasing look. "Is this Donald someone special?"

Lydia blushed. "He's just a patient."

"He is, is he?" Mother said, giving Lydia a long look. Larry figured that Mother was simply pleased Lydia was interested in someone. The whole family had been understanding but disappointed when Lydia and her longtime friend Truman Vaught had decided not to court when he returned from the war.

In spite of Lydia's denials, for the rest of the evening, Larry and Gloria teased Lydia about being sweet on her patients while she showed them how to make a scrapbook.

Chapter 10
A Dangerous Game

Larry laid in bed and stared at the ceiling when he woke up the next morning. He didn't feel like getting up. *It's just going to be another boring day at home.* At least they were able to sleep in a little longer since they didn't have school.

Harry rolled over in the bed on the other side of the room. "I wish Lydia would show movies on our ceiling like she does at the hospital."

Larry laughed. "Me, too!" He was in a better mood when they went downstairs for breakfast.

Mother's hotcakes tasted good on the cold December morning. Breakfast was interrupted by a knock on the front door.

"That must be Mr. Walton, the milkman." Mother stood beside the stove with a spatula in her hand, making more hotcakes. "Larry, would you tell him we need four pints of milk, a pound of butter, and a dozen eggs?"

Larry didn't like leaving his warm hotcakes, but it was always nice to see Mr. Walton. He was about Father's age, tall and skinny, and he was always cheerful.

"Morning, Larry. Look at that gray sky. Looks like there's snow in those clouds, and some snowmen and sledding, too."

Larry grinned. Only Mr. Walton would imagine snowmen and sleds falling with snowflakes from the sky.

Mr. Walton was walking down the walk to his horse-drawn wagon when Jack and Mabel passed him. Larry watched in surprise when they turned in at his house instead of continuing on to school.

"Did you forget Father won't let Gloria and me go to school today?" he asked when they reached the porch.

"Nope." Jack smiled. "They closed the schools again because of the Old Spanish Lady. They won't be open until January first, at least. So we thought we'd come over and see you and Glory."

"Great!" *Maybe today won't be so boring after all,* Larry thought. "You can help me carry this milk to the kitchen." He handed Jack two glass milk bottles and then gave Mabel a wire basket of eggs and the butter.

The day was much more fun spent with friends. Mr. Walton was wrong about the snow. It didn't snow at all. Even though it was cool outside, Jack and Larry played fighter aces in the backyard. They had two boards tied in the middle to thick branches of a large oak tree. In their imaginations, the tree became a fighter plane in the Great War.

Gloria and Mabel stayed indoors and made cloth bags and more storybooks for the veterans at Fort Snelling. Larry was glad that most of the time Harry played with the girls. He didn't like watching his younger brother when he had friends his own age to play with.

Larry and Jack had just wiped out the Kaiser's Red Baron when Gloria came outside.

"Enemy off your right wing!" Jack called to Larry, pointing at Gloria.

Larry opened his mouth to tell her not to bother them. Then he saw how upset she looked. He hung on to the rope with one hand, a toy rifle in the other, and let the board he was standing on swing back and forth beneath him. "What's wrong?"

"Mabel is crying." Gloria clutched her arms over her new military-style coat.

"Why?"

"Harry is playing with us. He keeps asking Mabel why Charlie can't come and play. Mother tried to explain to him that Charlie is in heaven now, but Harry doesn't understand."

Larry felt sorry for Mabel, but he didn't know what he could do.

Gloria bit her bottom lip. Then she asked, "Would you let Harry play with you for a while to keep him away from Mabel?"

Larry bit back a groan. He and Jack had been having a great time. Harry would ruin everything! But he didn't want Mabel to cry. "Sure."

He swung himself off the board and dropped to the ground, then followed her into the house. Nothing was the same anymore because of that old flu!

Aunt Anna and Uncle Hans, Lydia and her fifteen-year-old

brother Carl and twelve-year-old sister Edie came for dinner that night. It was the first time their families had been together since before Armistice Day.

"It's been too long since we've seen you!" Mother gave Aunt Anna a big hug.

Aunt Anna shook her head. "It seems no one visits like they used to with the flu epidemic this fall and winter. Everyone's afraid their friends and relatives will make them ill or worse. It's an awful thing to be afraid of the people you love most."

Mother agreed.

Larry and Gloria liked when the Schmidts visited. The girls were fun, and Larry thought Carl always had interesting stories to tell.

"Have you started the gifts for the veterans yet?" Lydia asked.

"We done lots!" Harry grinned up at her. "Want to see?"

"Sure!"

Gloria and Harry showed Lydia and Edie the bags and storybooks they'd been working on. Lydia and Edie bent their heads together, Lydia's straight blond hair next to Edie's brown curls, over one of the storybooks, laughing at the jokes.

"You're doing a great job," Lydia told Glory and Harry. "The vets will be so glad to get them."

Harry was so proud of her praise that his grin filled his whole face, and his little chest stuck out until Larry was sure his shirt buttons would pop off.

"I've been making some things, too," Edie said. "It's nice to have something to do when we're not in school and haven't been able to go to Red Cross work because of the flu."

"Now that we've had the flu," Lydia told her, "you should

be able to get back to work for the Red Cross. You won't be catching or spreading the flu anymore."

"Good!" Edie's blue eyes flashed with pleasure.

Gloria sighed. "I wish we'd had the flu already so we could go more places."

Everyone laughed. But Edie said, "No, you don't, Glory. The flu feels real bad!"

Larry sat on the floor, his arms about his knees, and listened eagerly as Carl told of his summer adventures on a farm south of Minneapolis. With so many men away at war, Carl and other students had been needed to help on the farms.

"Wow!" Larry burst out. "Wish I could have gone with you."

Carl brushed his straight dark hair from his forehead. "It was a lot of hard work. And a lot of people didn't like me or the Mennonite farmers who lived nearby because of our German names."

"I know, but at least you got to do something different. Don't you get bored with school closed and everything?"

Excitement lit up Carl's blue eyes. "I have a new job while the schools are closed."

"A job?" Jealousy flared through Larry. Carl always seemed to be doing something fun. He wished he was almost fifteen like Carl! "What kind of job?"

"The YMCA has arranged playground schedules at the schools while the schools are closed. Twice a week, each playground will have football, soccer, or some other sport organized. They've hired older boys, like me, to be boy leaders."

Gloria piped up. "It sounds to me like all the games are for boys again. It's not fair!"

"At least we have the bags and storybooks to work on for the veterans," Edie reminded her.

"I want to play football!" Harry kicked an imaginary ball as hard as he could. "Oof!" He fell right on his bottom in the middle of the parlor. His large dark eyes opened wide in surprise. His mouth opened in a large *0*.

Everyone laughed. In a moment, Harry was laughing with them, louder than anyone.

Liking the attention, Harry jumped up and hurried over to the piano stool. He set it spinning, grabbed on, and spun with it.

Mother grabbed him about the waist, stopping his antics. "Let's sing some songs," Mother said. "We can start with your favorite one, Harry." She sat down on the piano stool before he could claim it for another spin. The two families gathered about her and quickly joined in:

> "K–K–K–Katy, beautiful Katy,
>   She's the only g–g–g–girl that I adore.
> When the m-moon shines,
>   Over the cow shed,
> She'll be waiting at the k–k–k–kitchen door!"

Harry sang at the top of his lungs, loving the stuttering.

During the next song, Larry asked Carl for a schedule of the game times at the schools. He definitely planned to do some playing with his friends!

"But Father! All the boys will be going!" Larry couldn't believe Father had found still another place Larry couldn't go to have fun.

"I can't stop the other boys," Father said. "But I don't want you playing at these YMCA games at the schoolyards."

"But it's outside in the fresh air, Father. I haven't caught the flu yet, not at school, or the flickers, or doing Boy Scout work. I bet I won't catch it at all." Larry tried to keep his voice calm. Inside, his chest was filled with anger.

"I don't want you taking any unnecessary chances. We already talked about how important this is once. I don't even like to see you playing with Jack. He hasn't had the flu, either, so you could catch it from him. But I know you need to spend time with someone other than Glory and Harry.

"Now, I've got to get to the hospital. Help your mother out with Harry and chores around the house today, will you?"

Larry crossed his arms over his chest and glared at the floor. "Sure."

Father will never know, he told himself later as he and Jack hurried across the schoolyard toward the group of boys they saw gathered.

Carl greeted him with a warm hand clasp. "Glad you made it! I wasn't sure your father would let you come."

Larry just smiled at him. He didn't want to come right out and lie.

Like always, Larry had worn his mask when he left the house, telling Mother he was going to see Jack. None of the other boys were wearing masks. He could see the white strings of a couple masks sticking out of some of the boys' pockets.

While Carl started the boys choosing teams for football, Larry slipped off his mask and stuck it into his own pocket. Guilt and anger mixed together inside him, making his chest tight.

Father will never know, he repeated to himself, running over to stand with the team that had just chosen him for their side.

CHAPTER 11

The French Orphans

"Hi, Larry and Jack! Look how much money we collected!" Gloria and Mabel grinned as Gloria poured coins from the white stocking onto the kitchen table. Coins clattered and rolled. Larry caught a dime as it fell off the table's edge.

Jack picked a nickel out of the crumbs of his molasses cookie.

Sugar wasn't as limited as before, but Mother was saving all of it she could for Christmas baking. Larry didn't mind. He liked the molasses cookies. Today's newspaper said that the sugar rationed for the war just by Minnesotans during the last year had saved thirty-six million pounds of sugar for the Allies.

"What's the money for?" he mumbled around a bite of cookie.

"The Fatherless Children of France collection." Gloria started sorting the coins into piles of dimes, nickels, and pennies. "We would have collected more, but Father only let us go to people we knew had already had the flu."

Mabel held out both hands, palms up. She smiled at the boys. "Don't you two want to give some money? It only takes a dime to feed a child in France for one day."

"Sure, I'll give," Jack said, "but I don't have my money with me right now."

"I'll give, too," Larry said. "Now that the war is over, it seems like the next thing we need to do is take care of the people in the countries where the war was fought, like Belgium and France. I read in the newspaper there're lots of orphans because of the war."

Gloria was putting the coins in neat piles. "We asked Mother to take us down to the French Orphan Shop on Nicollet Avenue, but she can't. Father doesn't want her to go where there are people who might have the flu."

"That's where we have to take the money," Mabel explained. "They have a Christmas tree in the window. The decorations on the tree show how much money has been collected: a blue strip means $1, a read strip means $5. Silver stars mean $36.50. That's enough to care for one French orphan for a year."

"How much did you collect?" Larry asked, reaching for another brown cookie.

Gloria counted the coins aloud. "Three dollars and fifteen

cents." Disappointment dripped from her voice. "After all that work and all these dimes and nickels and pennies, I was sure we'd have at least five dollars."

Larry waved a hand at the coins. "Cheer up. You have enough for three blue strips. That means you'll have three decorations on the tree, not just one old red strip, like you'd have if you collected five dollars."

"That's true." Gloria's face brightened. "I'd really like to see the Christmas tree, wouldn't you, Mabel?"

Mabel nodded.

"Why don't you ask Lydia to take you down there?" Larry shrugged. "She doesn't have to worry about the flu anymore. I bet she'll take you if the shop is open during hours she isn't working at Fort Snelling."

The door between the kitchen and hall swung open, and Mother came into the kitchen. "Who will take whom to what shop?" She flashed a curious smile at them.

Gloria explained.

Mother's brow wrinkled in a worried frown. "I'm not sure you should go, Gloria. You haven't had the flu, either."

"But, Mother, we went to so much work collecting the money! I really want to see the tree."

Mother pressed her lips together and looked from the money to the girls and back to the money again. "I admit it doesn't seem fair not to let you see the tree after all your work. If Lydia agrees to take you and you *promise* not to touch anyone or talk to anyone else and to wear your mask every moment, you may go to the shop, Gloria."

Gloria and Mabel grabbed hands and jumped up and down, cheering.

Larry was glad for them, but he wished he could talk

Mother and Father into letting him go places as easily as Gloria could!

Gloria turned to the boys, holding out her hands as Mabel had done a few minutes earlier. "Pay up, boys!"

They laughed as they went to get their donations to the girls' collection.

Be quiet! Larry yelled silently at his guilty conscience the next morning as he followed Jack off a colorful yellow trolley at the train station.

Larry noticed only a few people in the crowd were wearing the familiar white mask. His own was stuck deep in one of his jacket pockets.

The 151st, or Rainbow Division, that Greg fought with wasn't returning yet. Most of the Minnesota men in the army were in the 151st. But Minnesota men who fought with other regiments were returning. Jack had heard that a large group of them were traveling through Minneapolis on the train today.

"Looks like you were right," Larry hollered at Jack over the noise of the crowd and the sound of trains entering and leaving the station.

Men and women so crowded the station that it was hard to walk. These people didn't know any of the men passing through to their homes in other parts of Minnesota. Just the same, they were talking to each other about "our boys" returning from the war. Happiness and excitement filled their faces.

The Home Folks of the 151st Regiment—made up of families of the soldiers—had a long line of tables set up. They had breakfast ready to serve the returning soldiers when the train stopped.

The first train with returning doughboys roared into the

station minutes after Larry and Jack arrived. Cheers from the people almost raised the station's roof.

Larry hollered and waved his hat with the rest of the crowd. *Why, I can't even hear myself!* he realized, and laughed until his face hurt.

Soldiers leaned out windows, shouting and waving back at the people in the station. They were all dressed in khaki uniforms with the service chevron on their chests.

The noise dimmed enough so that Larry could hear people if they talked loud. Larry and Jack shoved their way past men in business suits, factory workers in denim overalls, women in fancy coats and hats with fur muffs for their hands, and women in ragged wool coats.

When Larry and Jack finally reached the area near the tables, Larry poked Jack in the ribs with his elbow and pointed. "Look at the breakfast they're serving!"

Larry wasn't surprised to see the coffee and doughnuts. It was the candy and ice cream and ice cream sodas that surprised him!

The doughboys didn't seem to mind if the breakfast was unusual. They gladly accepted the food that was offered them. Larry thought there was a smile on every soldier's face.

Men and women in the station went up and shook hands with these soldiers they didn't know. Larry heard lots of them thanking the soldiers. He even saw a few businessmen and factory workers with tears running down their faces as they talked to the doughboys.

Larry blinked back tears that burned in his eyes. These soldiers had been through a lot!

He noticed Jack wipe a tear from his own cheek, but pretended he didn't see it.

Thirty thousand United States soldiers were being sent home every day now, Larry remembered. Surely before long the 151st would be coming. With almost 1,800,000 soldiers, the army couldn't send all the doughboys and jackies home at once! There wouldn't be room on all the ships and trains for them.

Larry and Jack and almost everyone else in the station house waited until the train left and watched it until it was out of sight. Soldiers leaned out the window as it steamed slowly out of the station, waving their khaki hats and shouting their thanks.

When he and Jack were back on a trolley, swaying with the car's movement, Larry said, "I wish it had been the 151st. I wish Greg had been on that train."

"Me, too." Jack's voice sounded gruff. He turned and looked out the window, and Larry couldn't see his face.

Every day in the Minneapolis *Tribune* there were more pictures of soldiers and sailors who had died since Armistice Day. Some died of battle wounds and some of the flu. Every time Larry saw the pictures, he thought of Greg and wondered if his picture would be in the next newspaper. He knew Jack wondered the same thing.

Half an hour after Larry got home, there was a pounding on the front door.

"Hold down the racket!" he called, hurrying from the kitchen where he and Glory and Harry were working on more storybooks for the vets. "I'm coming!"

Through the front door's frosted glass panel, he was surprised to see Jack.

When he opened the door, Jack waved a letter in front of his face. "He's alive! Greg's alive!"

Larry grinned. Happiness swelled up in his chest. Greg would be coming home! "You got a letter from him finally!"

Jack laughed. "We got lots of letters from him. They must have been lost somewhere or something. There's about ten letters." He grabbed Larry's shoulders and shook them. "He's alive!"

Two days later, Larry covered his head with his blanket when Mother came into the room to get him up.

"Come on, Lazybones. Rise and shine. Everyone else has already eaten breakfast." She tugged gently at the blanket.

"My head hurts." Larry groaned. "It hurts real bad."

Mother pulled the blanket down enough to hold the back of her hand against his head. "I think you have a fever."

Larry shut his eyes against the morning sunshine. The light made his head hurt even more. "I don't want breakfast."

He stayed in bed all morning. By noon he felt worse than he'd ever felt in his life.

"It feels like my bones hurt," he told Mother. "They ache something fierce."

"I'll heat some blankets. Maybe that will help. Father will probably have some medicine with him when he gets home."

She sounded worried. Larry opened his eyes and squinted up at her. Her eyes looked worried, too.

"What's wrong with me?" he asked.

"I'm afraid it's the flu, Larry. You have the flu."

CHAPTER 12

The Flu Hits Home

The warm blankets felt good and eased the aching in Larry's legs and hips a bit, but they didn't take it away.

"I feel like some bully beat me up with a big board," he told Mother.

Mother had given him special care all day. She'd wiped his face with a cool cloth when he was hot and brought him water.

For lunch, Mother brought him chicken soup, but he wasn't hungry. He usually liked Mother's chicken soup, but today the smell made him feel worse. Mother tried to prop up his pillows and get him to eat. He turned his head away. "I'm not hungry."

Harry leaned his forearms on Larry's bed. "Do you want me to read you a story, Larry?"

"No."

"I can make you a storybook."

"No."

"I can sing you a song. 'K-k-k-Katy! Beautiful Katy!' "

Larry clapped his hands over his ears. "Stop it! Go away!"

"Harry is only trying to make you feel better," Mother said in her soft voice.

Larry knew that, but he felt so bad that it took too much energy to be nice to Harry.

Mother filled a spoon with soup and held it to his lips.

Larry turned his head away. "I don't want any. I just want to sleep and wake up when the flu is over and I feel better."

Mother sighed and stood up. "All right. Come along, Harry."

Harry rubbed a hand back and forth on his forehead. His face screwed into wrinkles like he was going to cry. "Mother, my head hurts."

It wasn't long before Harry was in bed, too.

By the time Father came home for the evening meal, Gloria was in bed.

Father went from one bed to another. He put a thermometer in Larry's mouth. Larry was shivering so hard he thought he might bite right through the thermometer. He wondered what his temperature was. Only doctors and nurses had thermometers, so he hadn't had his temperature taken earlier.

Father looked at the thermometer. "Let's see—102 degrees. Headache, aching muscles. You have the flu, all right."

"I hurt a lot. D. . .don't you have s. . .some m. . .medicine for it?"

"I'll give you some aspirin powders. They will make you

feel a little better, but they won't stop the flu. Warm food, warm blankets, lots of liquids, and lots of sleep. That's the best medicine."

"I'm so c–cold. Can I have more b–blankets?" He already had three, but he was still cold.

"I'll get another one for you. Mother tells me you didn't have any of her soup at lunch."

"I didn't want to eat. I wasn't h. . .hungry."

"You need to eat warm foods and drink water to get better."

"C–can we shut the window?"

It was only open a couple inches, but the wind blew the December cold into the room.

Father shook his head. "Sorry, Son, but you know how important it is to have fresh air."

"Papa," Harry whined from his bed across the room, "I hurt."

Father went over and brushed Harry's hair off his forehead. "I know. I'll bring you some aspirin powders, too, after I check on Glory. Try to sleep. Mother's bringing you another nice warm blanket. She's steaming it down in the kitchen right now."

"No, I'm not. I'm here." Mother walked into the room carrying a blue wool blanket over a wooden rod. "I have a nice warm blanket for you, Harry."

Larry watched through sore eyes while Mother and Father wrapped the warm blanket around Harry. "That should help your aches a bit, Son," Father said.

Mother leaned against the door frame, watching Father. He stopped beside her. "You look tired, Frances. Your cheeks are flushed. Are you sure you haven't come down with it yourself?"

"I'm fine. Just tired from taking care of the children." She rubbed her forehead.

"Do you have a headache?" Father asked sharply.

"Yes, but I'm sure it's only from being tired."

"More likely it's the flu. I want you to go to bed right now." Larry could hear the fear in Father's voice.

Mother shook her head, brushing strands of hair off her face. "I have another blanket steaming downstairs for Gloria, and I'm making soup for everyone."

"If you have the flu, it will only make it worse if you work instead of rest."

Mother waved a hand toward Larry. "Look at poor Larry. The boy is shivering. I should steam another blanket for him, too."

"In five minutes, he'll probably be sweating. Warm blankets help the muscle aches more than the chills."

Larry thought a warm blanket sounded nice, but he was too tired and sick to argue with Father.

"Frances, you know how important it is for you to take care of yourself now that you've been exposed to the flu," Father said sternly. "I want you to go to bed."

"I'm not going to bed when our children need me, Richard," Mother answered quietly.

Father planted his hands on his hips. "You can be so stubborn sometimes! I'll ask Mabel's mother to look after the children. She and her entire family have had the flu. She can't catch it again. If she comes, will you go to bed?"

"Maybe."

Mother stood up straight. "I'd better check on the blanket for Gloria and on the soup." She pressed a hand against her back. "Oooh!"

Father grabbed her arm. "What is it?"

"I'm not sure. It started aching just now, like a headache, only in my back."

Father's lips pinched together. "The flu. That's it. You're going to bed."

"But—"

"No buts, Frances. As soon as you're in bed and you and the children have taken some aspirin powders, I'll go across the street and talk to Mabel's mother." He helped her down the hall.

Larry shut his eyes. *Mother can't be sick!* he thought desperately. *I couldn't have given her the flu. I couldn't have!*

Father dissolved aspirin powders in a glass of water for each of them. Larry thought it tasted terrible, but it helped his headache a little, and he slept better. His muscles still hurt, though.

One time during the night, Larry woke up with a bad headache again. His pajamas were soaked with sweat and so was he. When Father checked on him, Larry saw two of him, and both Fathers were fuzzy. Father gave him more aspirin powders in cool water and bathed his face with a damp, cold rag.

From across the room, Larry could hear Harry crying softly in his sleep. Larry felt like crying himself.

Dawn's light was coming in the window and birds were beginning to sing their morning songs when voices in the hall outside the bedroom woke Larry.

"Thanks for coming, Lydia." Father's voice sounded tired.

"I'm glad to be able to be here. There isn't much flu at the Fort Snelling Hospital now, and since I'm helping with the disabled veterans, I don't have to work around the clock."

"If you can help here while I work at City Hospital, it will put my mind at ease. It's hard to leave my family, but I do have a responsibility to my patients and the hospital."

"That's what family is for," Lydia said. "I wouldn't be a nurse now if it weren't for your example and Grandfather Allerton's."

"I asked Mabel's mother, from across the street, if she would help out. Her family had the flu last month. I explained she and her family can't catch it again, but she didn't believe me. I can't blame her for being frightened. She lost a daughter and a son to this awful flu."

"The poor dear!"

"She did offer to make soup and porridge and buy any fruit or other groceries you might need and leave them on the porch each day."

"That will help," Lydia said.

"In October and November, hardly any school-aged children were severely ill with this flu. No one that age died in Minneapolis. With the new wave of flu this month, almost half the new cases are among schoolchildren. I hate to think what is ahead for us and the rest of the city."

"We'll be praying."

"Yes," Father said wearily. "Yes, we will pray."

CHAPTER 13

Scary News

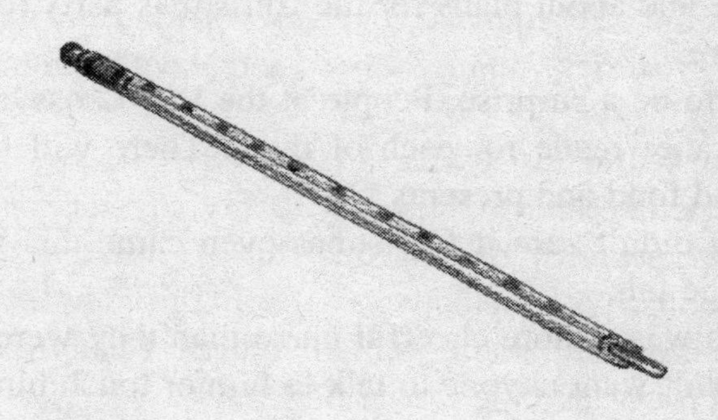

Larry had never felt so bad in his life. Father had been right about the aspirin powders. They made him feel a little better, but they didn't take all the pain away. He felt so bad that he couldn't believe he would ever feel better again. And now he had a short, hard cough, too.

Mother had asked Father to move her bed into the boys' bedroom so she could be near the children. Harry wanted to sleep beside Mother, so Gloria was in Harry's bed.

It would be like a big party, Larry thought, *if we didn't all feel so awful.*

Even though Larry knew Mother felt as bad as he and Glory and Harry, she was patient with them. She held Harry when he cried. When they were sweating with fever, she would bathe their heads and tell Lydia where to find clean, dry pajamas for them.

Lydia was a kind, cheerful nurse. She tried to keep them comfortable, heated their porridge and soups for meals, peeled oranges for them to suck on, washed their pajamas, heated blankets, gave them aspirin powders, and read them stories and newspapers.

She told them funny things the soldiers at Fort Snelling had done and about plans for the Christmas party for the soldiers there.

"It's to be a surprise. People at the Red Cross are having special canes made for each of them. There will be special music and food and presents."

Larry didn't care if Christmas even came this year—not the way he felt.

Lydia was a more cheerful nurse than they were patients. Larry didn't want anyone to talk to him or touch him. He just wanted to feel better!

By noon of the second day, everyone had the hacking cough Larry had developed during the night. "That's normal with this flu," Lydia told them.

Larry heard the telephone ring often. Lydia told them it was Father, calling from City Hospital to see how they were doing and to send his love.

When Father came home from the hospital each evening, he would check on each of the family. Then he would take a nap for a couple hours before Lydia left. Lydia would be back when Father left for the hospital in the morning.

For two days, Larry hurt so bad he didn't care about anything. He tried to read, but his eyes were too sore.

Then one morning his headache was gone. His muscles were still a little sore, but only like after a hard game of football. It didn't feel like his very bones were throbbing anymore. He still had his cough. Lydia told him that would go away after a few days.

Lydia took his temperature and grinned. "Your fever is gone. Great! You can take a bath if you want to, and I'll put fresh bedding on for you. Then you should go back to bed."

"But I feel so much better! I'm tired of being in bed. Can't I go downstairs?"

Lydia shook her head. "Sorry. People who don't stay in bed for a few days after their fever is over often have a relapse."

"What's a relapse?" Gloria asked from Harry's bed.

"That means a person gets sick all over again."

Larry waved his hands like an umpire waving a baseball player safe. "I don't want to go through that again! I'll stay in bed."

By noon, Gloria was feeling better, too.

A couple hours later, Larry and Gloria were restless. "Can't we play?" Larry begged Lydia.

"You can read. Maybe you'd like to put together a jigsaw puzzle. Lots of soldiers at the hospital enjoy putting them together."

"You could read the new Anne of Green Gables book you gave me for my birthday," Gloria offered.

"That's a girl's book!"

"It's got Gilbert Blythe in it," Gloria told him. "There are lots of boys' things in it to make it exciting."

"Well, I'll give it a try."

He read until he was too tired to read anymore. Even when

his eyes kept closing, he wanted to keep reading. It was one of the best stories he'd ever read, even if it was a girl's book.

"Why am I still so tired if I'm better?" he asked Lydia.

"Your body knows it needs lots of sleep to get back the strength it lost fighting the flu."

When he woke up, Father was home, sitting beside Gloria on Harry's bed. She was chattering away as though she'd never been sick at all. Larry thought she was probably glad to have all of Father's attention for a change.

Mother and Harry were still sleeping, though they were tossing restlessly. Father glanced their way with a worried expression on his face while he listened to Gloria.

Lydia had made a special supper for Larry and Gloria because they were feeling better. She brought trays up to the bedroom for them and for Father and herself, too.

"Real food!" Larry grinned at her when she handed him his tray. On it was buttered bread, mashed potatoes, chicken meat cut into small pieces, and a glass of milk. "I'm so hungry I could eat a horse."

"Me, too," Gloria chimed in.

"You shouldn't even finish all of this," Father said. "If you do, you won't be feeling well for long. Just try a few bites of each thing. Your body has to get used to eating something other than porridge and soup and oranges."

"There's a note on my tray!" Gloria unfolded it.

"Mabel brought it over," Lydia told her.

Gloria scanned it quickly. "She only says she misses me and hopes we'll all be better soon."

"It was kind of her to remember you that way," Father said. "I'm glad you have such a good friend."

Gloria beamed.

Father had been right. They weren't able to finish everything on their trays.

"But what I ate was wonderful." Larry rubbed his stomach. "Thanks, Lydia."

Mother woke up just then. Father hurried over to her side. She gave him a small smile while he brushed her bangs back off her forehead. Larry could see her bangs were wet. She must be sweating again.

"How are you feeling?" Father asked her.

"Not so wonderful."

Father turned to Lydia. "Where is the thermometer?"

Lydia found it and handed it to him.

"Would you make Frances up some aspirin powder water?" he asked Lydia after sticking the thermometer in Mother's mouth.

Larry frowned. Father seemed worried about Mother.

Father's lips pressed together hard when he looked at the thermometer.

Lydia held the glass of aspirin powder water to Mother's lips. "Are you hungry?"

Mother nodded. "A little. Is there any chicken soup?"

"Yes, Mabel's mother brought some over. I'll heat some for you." Lydia hurried away.

Mother gave Father a funny little smile. "I'm very tired of being sick, Doctor."

"Tired? When have you had this much attention?" Father grinned. "Usually you're the one taking care of everyone else. I suggest you enjoy all this service while you have the chance."

"Perhaps I should."

"Do you know Larry and Glory are feeling better? Their fevers have broken, and soon they'll be into trouble again."

Mother smiled over at Larry and Glory. Larry smiled back

and gave her a small wave. "I'm glad you're better."

She started coughing again. Her coughing woke Harry. Soon Father was taking his temperature and making up aspirin powder water for him, too.

Later, when Mother, Harry, and Gloria were resting again, Larry walked down the hall to the bathroom. It was at the top of the stairs. He could hear Lydia and Father speaking in the hallway below.

"I'm worried about Frances and Harry," Father was saying.

Worried about Mother and Harry? Father's words stopped Larry with one hand on the bathroom door. He held his breath until his chest hurt, trying to hear better.

"Their fevers should have started coming down by now," Father continued. "Three days is as long as the fever usually lasts if there aren't complications."

Complications? Does that mean the flu gets worse, like pneumonia? Larry wondered.

"Frances came down with the flu symptoms later than the children," Lydia said. "I'm sure her fever and Harry's will be down by morning."

Father sighed. "I hope so. Thanks for staying so long today, Lydia."

"I'll be back in the morning."

Larry heard the door close behind her. He stood leaning against the bathroom door, his heart racing. *In the morning. They'll be better in the morning. There's nothing to worry about.*

But they weren't better in the morning. Larry watched closely, praying hard, while Father took Mother and Harry's temperatures again. The strained, scared look on Father's face when he read the thermometers told Larry that instead of getting better, Mother and Harry were worse.

Chapter 14

Will Mother Live?

Fear seemed to seep into Larry's bones the way the flu had seeped into them. He ached with the fear, and he knew no aspirin powder water would help.

He'd brought the flu home because he'd played football with the other boys and gone to the train station when he knew Father wouldn't approve. He'd hidden his mask in his pocket when he was away from home. And now Mother and Harry were sick. Very sick. Sicker than Larry had been when he didn't think it was possible to feel any worse.

When Lydia arrived, she and Father whispered together out in the hall. Larry wished he knew what they were saying.

Father came back into the room. "I'm going back to the

hospital now. Larry and Gloria, since you're feeling better, maybe you can help Lydia today. She's going to be very busy taking care of Mother and Harry."

Larry and Gloria nodded.

Lydia took care of four of us before without any help, Larry thought. *Why does she need help now?* Fear twisted his stomach.

"Why don't you two go downstairs?" Lydia smiled at Larry and Gloria. "Maybe you can do a puzzle together, or maybe you'd like to finish the Anne of Green Gables book, Larry."

Larry looked at her in surprise. Yesterday she hadn't wanted them to go downstairs. She'd said they needed their rest.

Lydia must have noticed his look. "Your mother and Harry will rest better if you two play downstairs now that you're feeling stronger."

Larry couldn't get interested in Gloria's book again. He sat in the big oak rocking chair with the leather seat, the book lying in his lap, and stared out the window. Gloria sat beside a table on which a jigsaw puzzle was spread, but he didn't see her try to match even one piece. Finally she took her favorite doll, curled up in a corner of the sofa, and stared out the window with him.

Larry remembered Father and Uncle Erik talking about ladies like Mother who caught the flu, ladies who were expecting babies. It wasn't safe for them, Father had said. Sometimes the ladies died from the flu. Sometimes the unborn babies died, too.

Would Mother and their unborn brother or sister die?

The question kept going around and around in his head.

He was glad when Lydia came into the room and asked if they'd like to help her. "I've put clean sheets on your mother's bed," she said. "I'm going to boil them to get rid of any flu bacteria, so I'll be busy for a while in the kitchen. Will you sit with your mother and Harry?"

Mother and Harry were both very hot. Gloria and Larry wiped their faces and put cold cloths on their foreheads, as Mother had done for them when they were ill. They made aspirin powder water. Harry wouldn't take his water for Gloria. He pushed it away, scowling. "Tastes bad!"

Larry laughed. "He's right. It does taste bad."

"Please, Harry," Mother said in her soft voice, "drink it for Mother. It will help you feel better."

"No!"

"What about an orange slice?" Larry asked. "Wouldn't that taste good?"

Harry stared at him for a minute. Then he nodded.

"I'll get it for you." Usually they only had fresh fruit in the wintertime on special occasions. There was usually an orange in the toe of each of their Christmas stockings. It was almost a treat to have the oranges, even though they'd had to get sick to have them!

"Here's your orange, Harry," Larry said when he came back into the bedroom. "You can only have it if you drink your aspirin water."

"No!"

"Yes."

Finally Harry drank it.

Mother smiled at Larry, and he smiled back. He felt like he'd won the war, getting Harry to drink that water.

Harry grabbed for the orange slices. He only ate one slice. Larry had to clean up Harry's hands and face after he was done.

The aspirin water didn't seem to help Mother and Harry.

Their fevers continued to climb. Lydia's face grew more sober every time she took their temperature.

While Lydia and Gloria were making supper for everyone, Larry stayed with Mother and Harry. They were very hot, and Larry kept wiping their faces and hands with the cold rags. He wrung out other cold rags and placed them behind their necks, just as Lydia had shown him to do, to help bring down their temperatures.

While Larry was replacing the rag behind Harry's neck, Mother mumbled something.

"What? I didn't hear what you said."

She mumbled again. She didn't look at him. Her eyes were closed.

"What did you say, Mother?" He leaned closer to hear her better.

"They are all in the ditch."

Larry jerked up straight in surprise. "Ditch? What ditch? Who is in the ditch?"

"The pigs. They're in the ditch." She opened up her eyes and looked straight at him. "Orren, get the pigs out of the ditch. Father will be mad."

Orren is Mother's brother. Does she think I'm Orren? Is she having a nightmare? Larry wondered.

"Orren, look." Mother pointed to a light hanging from the middle of the ceiling. "It's snowing." She smiled at Larry. "I love the snow, don't you, Orren?"

Fright surged through Larry. Something was very wrong. He dashed from the room and tore down the hall to the stairway. "Lydia! Lydia, come quick!" he called.

He bolted down the stairway and ran smack into Father, who was walking in the front door. Panting, Larry grabbed

Father's shirt. "Something is wrong with Mother! She thinks I'm Uncle Orren."

Father's gaze met Lydia's. "Delusions?" Father's voice was tight and scared.

Lydia shook her head. "She was fine when I was up there last time. Her fever is still high, but nothing had changed."

They hurried up the stairs together. Larry stood on the bottom step with his hand on the stair post, staring after them. He didn't want to go back up there until Father made Mother better. It was too scary!

When Father and Lydia came back downstairs, Father used the telephone in the living room to call the hospital. Larry heard him ask if there were two beds open so he could bring his wife and son to the hospital.

Fear clutched at Larry's heart. *Father must think they are awfully sick if he wants to take them to the hospital!*

When he hung up, he looked at Lydia and shook his head. "There are no beds available. I knew that, but I hoped they would find some beds for me, anyway. We're swamped with flu patients at the hospital again. I haven't been working my fair share of time because of the illness here at home. I can't keep shirking my duty and letting other doctors work longer hours because of me. I'd hoped with Mother and Harry at the hospital, I could work the longer hours and still watch over them."

Lydia walked over and took the earphone off the hook. "I'll call Fort Snelling Hospital and tell them I won't be back until Aunt Frances and Harry are well."

"They need you at that hospital, too," Father protested, but Larry saw the look of hope in his tired eyes.

"They don't need me as much as Aunt Frances and Harry."

For the next two days, Lydia watched over Mother and

Harry most of the time, while Larry and Gloria took care of most of the things that needed to be done downstairs.

They steamed blankets, made meals, did the dishes, boiled sheets and handkerchiefs, and even boiled the eating utensils Mother and Harry used.

"I'm glad Mabel's mother is bringing us some food every day," Gloria said, carrying in a basket covered with a clean linen towel from the porch. "At least I don't have to cook everything. She brought cranberry bread today for you and me and Lydia. She must be doing Christmas baking."

"I'd forgotten all about Christmas!" Larry said. "Seems strange to think people are rushing around buying presents and going to parties, doesn't it? All I want for Christmas is for Mother and Harry to get well!"

"Me, too." Gloria brushed away a sudden tear. "Remember Mabel telling us how sometimes she took care of her whole family all by herself when they had the flu?"

Larry nodded. "I don't know how she did it. What would we have done without Lydia?"

"I wouldn't have known what to do. And I'm so tired, I can't hardly think about making supper." Gloria pulled out a white wooden kitchen chair and plopped into it. "I didn't know taking care of sick people was so much work. I wouldn't be a nurse for all the money in the world."

"I'm tired, too," Larry admitted. But he didn't mind all the hard work. Maybe if he worked hard enough for Mother and Harry, God wouldn't let them die. He wouldn't be able to stand it if they died, and it was his fault!

The next day, Lydia asked Larry to watch Mother and Harry for her while she took a nap. Lydia had been up most of the night watching the patients.

Lydia placed a hand on Larry's shoulder. "I think the delusions are over. The fevers are down slightly, and Aunt Frances and Harry are resting quietly now, except for their coughs."

The tightness in Larry's chest loosened. So Lydia had known how afraid he'd been of Mother's strange talk.

"You might bring some orange slices up for them."

"All right." Larry turned to get the oranges from the kitchen.

"If. . ." Lydia hesitated.

Larry looked back at her. "Yes?"

Lydia bit her bottom lip, then said in a rush. "If you notice any pink stains on your mother or Harry's handkerchiefs after they cough or. . .or anything, let me know, okay?"

"Sure." What would that mean? Larry wanted to ask. He didn't dare put the question into words.

Mother's breathing was short, almost like panting. She seemed too tired to hold the orange slices herself. Larry held one to her lips, and she sucked on it. "The juice tastes good. Thank you," she whispered. She smiled at him, a small smile.

"Can I do anything else for you?"

"Tell me what you and Gloria have been doing." Her words came slow and soft.

"Just helping Lydia with the cooking and cleaning and laundry and stuff."

"My, my." *Cough.* "You will be all trained in by the time I'm out of bed again." *Cough.* "I'll be able to be a lady of leisure."

"You sure will." Larry grinned at her. He'd do housework and laundry for the rest of his life if she wanted him to, if it would make her get better.

She patted his hand. "You're a good boy, Larry, a good son."

His lips quivered, but he kept smiling. *She wouldn't think I was a good son if she knew I brought the flu home because I did things I wasn't supposed to do!*

Mother started coughing again and couldn't seem to quit. Larry handed her a clean handkerchief from the bureau drawer. When she was done coughing, he held a glass of water to her lips so she could have a drink.

"Thank you," she whispered when she was done. She put her head back against the pillow and closed her eyes. "I think I'll sleep for a bit now."

Larry put the glass back on the table beside the bed. Then he straightened the blankets. That was when he saw the pink stains on the handkerchief.

His hands froze on top of the blanket. *Pink stains!* What did they mean?

He hurried into Gloria's bedroom where Lydia was napping and shook her shoulder. "Wake up!"

Lydia squinted up at him. "What is it, Larry?"

"Pink stains. I saw the pink stains."

Lydia was off the bed in a flash. She checked on Mother to see for herself the stains Larry told her about. Then she ran down the hall and stairs.

Larry followed on her heels to the kitchen. She went right to the telephone and rang up City Hospital. Whoever answered told her Dr. Allerton was too busy to talk to her now.

"You listen to me," Lydia said in a hard, grown-up tone Larry had never heard her use before. "This is the woman nursing his wife and son. You tell him his wife has pneumonia, and you tell him right now!"

Pneumonia! Larry gripped the back of a chair, hard. *People die from pneumonia! That's what Father told Uncle Erik. They die!*

CHAPTER 15

An Unusual Christmas

Father was home within an hour. He raced up the stairs to Mother's side without even saying hello to Larry and Gloria, who met him in the downstairs hall.

Larry had never seen his father look so frightened. He'd always thought Father could handle anything! *If Father is that scared, Mother must be in awful danger,* he thought.

Gloria took hold of his hand. "Are you sure Lydia said *pneumonia*?"

"Yes, and quit whispering."

"You're whispering," she whispered back.

He shook off her hand and went into the parlor. He sat down in the corner of the sofa and drew his knees close to his chest. Mother wouldn't like it if she knew he had his shoes on the sofa, but he didn't take them off. He just stared at the floor, trying to stop the fear and hurt inside him.

Gloria sat down next to him, snuggling up against him. "A girl at school told me half the people who get pneumonia from the Spanish flu die. Is that true, Larry?"

Half! The terror inside him tightened like a screw until he wanted to scream.

"Is it true, Larry?" Gloria repeated.

"I don't know. How would I know? Don't talk to me!"

Tears brimmed in Gloria's eyes. "B. . .but I'm scared."

"I'm scared, too."

"Let's pray for Mother and Harry." She reached for his hand.

He held hands with her while she prayed, repeating the words silently in his own mind. When they were done, he couldn't help remembering Violet and Charlie. They'd prayed for Mabel's family when they were sick. If Violet and Charlie died, Mother and Harry could die, too.

"I'm glad Father is a doctor," Gloria said. "I used to be mad when Father worked so hard taking care of sick people. Now that I know how hard and scary it is to take care of sick people, I think I understand why he works so hard to help them. It must be awful to be sick if your father isn't a doctor, don't you think?"

"I never thought about it before, but I guess you're right."

Father didn't go back to the hospital that night, or the next day, or the next night, or the day after that. He stayed in the room with Mother and Harry almost all the time. He even slept there.

For Harry had developed pneumonia, too.

Mother and Harry were too sick to visit with family. Gloria was sleeping in her own bedroom, sharing it with Lydia. Larry's bed had been moved to Mother and Father's room.

Larry and Gloria would stand at the bedroom door and look in at Mother and Harry. The two lay against the pillows, their faces gray, and coughed and coughed.

I'm sorry, God, Larry would pray silently, watching them. *Please forgive me and save them.*

Larry's chest felt crushed under the terror and guilt, like someone had set a hundred-pound rock on his chest that he couldn't push off. It hurt worse than the flu had hurt.

If they don't get better, I'll hurt like this for the rest of my life.

"Is there any medicine for pneumonia?" Larry asked Lydia one day.

"Quinine. Your father has given that to your mother and Harry." She rested a hand on his shoulder. "Your father is a very good doctor. Aunt Frances and Harry couldn't have better care."

But even the best doctors can't save everybody, he thought.

Larry would never have believed a house could be so quiet with six people in it. They hardly spoke to each other. No one had anything to say except how scared they were. Everyone did what they had to do, but they didn't talk much.

And then one morning, Father came into the room where Larry slept. Father's shoulders sagged with weariness beneath his shirt. His eyes were rimmed in red from so many nights without sleep. But he was wearing a huge smile.

"They're going to make it, Larry. They're going to make it!"

Father gave Larry a bear hug and then went to tell Gloria.

Larry buried his head in his pillow and cried in relief. *Thank You, God! Thank You for saving them.*

When Larry came downstairs for breakfast, Father was closing the front door behind him. "Where is he going?" he asked Lydia. "Back to the hospital?"

She smiled mysteriously and set a bowl of oatmeal and raisins in front of him. "You'll see."

An hour later, Father was back. He walked into the parlor where Larry and Gloria were reading. He was carrying a scraggly looking evergreen tree and wearing a huge grin. "Merry Christmas!"

Larry's jaw dropped. "I forgot. I forgot it's Christmas!"

Chapter 16
Bird Day

Although Mother and Harry were out of danger, they were still very ill and tired. They stayed in bed and slept a lot.

The day after Christmas, Larry removed the quarantine sign from the front door. It could have been removed sooner, Father said, but he'd forgotten about it.

"At least there are no black crepe bows on our door," Larry muttered, taking down the sign.

"Larry! Hi!"

Larry turned with a grin to meet Jack. He hadn't seen him

since the day they went to the train station together.

"I guess everyone at your house must be over the flu if you're taking down the sign."

Larry nodded. "Finally!"

"We had the flu at our house, too," Jack told him, "but we were over it a lot sooner than the people at your house. Mabel told me your mother and Harry got pneumonia. That didn't happen to anyone at our house."

"I'm glad. It was pretty rough stuff."

"Want to go to the park this afternoon? The ice rink opened there last week."

"Great!"

It was fun to get outside and do something with a friend again. Larry and Jack belted their skate blades around their boots and headed out on the ice. It took a few minutes and a few falls to get the hang of skating again.

When they were done, they hung their blades over their shoulders and strolled through the park. A blue bird darted past, startling them, and lighted on an evergreen bough.

Jack pulled his slingshot from his pocket. He pushed at the snow with the toe of his boot, searching for a stone. When he found one and stood up to take aim, the bird darted off.

"Shoot! Too late."

Larry noticed someone coming toward them. "Here comes a policeman! Better hide your sling."

Jack slid it into his coat pocket, keeping his mittened hand in his pocket, too.

The officer stopped beside them, grinning. The sunshine shone off the bright brass buttons on his coat.

Larry's heart raced. Had he seen Jack's slingshot? Would he take it away from him?

The officer reached out and touched the tip of one of Jack's skate blades with a finger. "Been skating, I see. How's the ice?"

"Great!" Jack said, giving the officer his one-sided smile. "It's still smooth. After a couple thaws and refreezes, we'll have some bumps to skate around, I suppose."

"Oh, I remember those days!" The officer rocked back and forth on his boots. "I used to love skating when I was your age. Good sport!"

"Yes," the boys agreed at the same time.

Another blue jay, or maybe the same one, landed on a branch above them. The branch bounced, spraying them with snow, while the bird chattered at them.

Larry and Jack looked at each other and burst out laughing. The policeman laughed, too. Then he touched his fingers to his hat and left. The bird took off, too.

"Whew!" Jack took off his hat and wiped the back of his hand across his forehead. "That was close."

"That's probably what that blue jay is thinking."

Jack laughed.

Larry was glad the policeman hadn't taken Jack's slingshot, but he was glad Jack hadn't killed the bird, either. With a start, he realized he didn't want to kill birds anymore. After Mother and Harry came so close to dying, he never wanted to kill anything again.

The first day back to school in January, the temperatures were below zero, but it was warm in the classroom. Larry and Jack and Gloria and Mabel were excited to get back, until they discovered how school had changed.

The classrooms weren't filled with students. Many were out with the flu. About half as many as had the flu had been kept home by parents who were afraid they would catch the flu.

And there were more empty desks that used to seat children who had become orphans because the flu had killed their parents. Those children wouldn't be back. Larry wondered where each of them was and if he'd ever see them again. Or had the Old Spanish Lady taken them out of his life forever?

"Because we've all missed so much school," Miss Wilson told them, "classes will be changed for the rest of the year."

"How?" Larry asked, raising his hand.

"Unnecessary classes will be removed so we will have time to make up the things we missed in the most important classes, like reading and arithmetic and geography."

Larry raised his hand again. "I guess unnecessary classes means the fun classes, like physical education."

Miss Wilson shook her head, her eyes sparkling, a smile on her skinny face. "I'm afraid so, Larry."

A large groan went up from the class.

Miss Wilson held up a hand. "We're going to be studying exciting things, too. We'll be studying the New World Era we're entering, the new time for the world that's been won by our noble soldiers in the Great War. Thanks to them, we're entering a time of peace in the world, and democracy, and building, and countries working together instead of against each other. It's a great time to be alive."

Larry thought so, too, now that they knew Greg would be coming back from the war and that Mother and Harry wouldn't die from the flu.

A couple weeks later, Larry and Jack exchanged surprised looks when the policeman that almost caught Jack with his slingshot in the park came into class. Miss Wilson introduced him as Officer Tubbs. "He is going to spend the day with us."

"You might have heard about the ban on slingshots," Officer Tubbs started.

The boys in the class groaned and nodded.

"Yes, I thought so. The other officers and I have been concerned with all the birds being killed by boys in Minneapolis parks this fall and winter. We've stopped a number of boys with gunny sacks filled with songbirds they've killed with slingshots and BB guns."

Larry shifted uneasily in his seat. He heard Jack doing the same in the desk behind him.

"We've been afraid," Officer Tubbs continued, "that because of the war, children no longer place any value on life. War is full of violence, it's true. But the reason our friends and brothers and sons and fathers fought in the Great War was to protect the value of life. All life."

Larry shifted again. He could see other boys who looked as guilty as he felt.

Officer Tubbs grinned. "We policemen have worked with the schools to make today Bird Day. We're going to learn what the different birds contribute to our parks and lives here in Minneapolis. And we're going to do something to pay the birds back for the harm that's been done to them this year. We're going to make birdhouses."

The day was a lot more fun than Larry expected. He carried his wooden birdhouse home, eager to show it to his parents and Harry.

Harry was singing "K–K–K–Katy" at the top of his lungs when Larry entered the kitchen. He was glad his little brother was feeling good enough to sing, but he shook his head at him.

"I'm tired of singing. Our principal's new school slogan is *Sing*."

"What kind of slogan is that?" Mother asked, placing cookies on a plate and offering him one.

"A strange one." Larry puffed out his chest and tried to copy the principal. " 'When a class needs waking up, make it sing. If the class is too noisy, quiet them by singing a dignified song. Let them sing changing rooms. Let them sing when school is dismissed.' "

Mother laughed. "No wonder you're tired of singing."

Harry leaned his elbows against the kitchen table and looked up at Larry with big brown eyes. "Do you sing 'K–K–K–Katy'?"

"Sometimes."

Harry pointed a stubby finger at the birdhouse. "What's that?"

Larry told them, proud of the good job he'd done on the birdhouse. "I thought I'd hang it in the oak tree in the backyard."

"Fine," Mother agreed. She grinned at him. "I have some good news today, too. Have you seen the newspaper yet?"

Larry shook his head.

Mother picked up the paper and held it so he could see the big, bold headline that covered the top of the paper: UNITED STATES FIRST GREAT NATION OF THE WORLD TO GO DRY.

"We went dry? Does that mean the prohibition amendment has been ratified and is a law now?"

"Yes, but the law doesn't go into effect for a year."

"Guess you'll have to stop wearing your prohibition pins," Larry teased. His favorite was the one that said, "Bread not beer."

He pointed to another article on the front page. "What is this about the Minnesota suffragists?"

Mother snapped the paper. "Oh, that article made me so mad! There was a big meeting of suffragists in Washington, D.C., to try to convince senators to vote for the nineteenth amendment. They held a demonstration near the Lincoln Memorial and had simple, well-contained fires in cans as part of the demonstration. They were arrested. Then during the trial, three of my friends from Minneapolis were arrested!"

"What did they do?" Larry was horrified. He couldn't imagine any of his mother's friends as jailbirds.

"All they did was applaud the other suffragists during their trial." Mother held up her hands. Her usually calm eyes snapped with anger. "They clapped their hands, and for that, they spent twenty-four hours in jail. The indignity of it!"

Larry laughed. His mother's friends weren't such dangerous people after all. "I guess you really are feeling better if you're getting excited over prohibition and suffragist activities again."

She laughed and stuck her hands in her apron pockets. "I am at that and thankful to be well."

Larry was thankful she was well, too, but he still felt guilty for bringing the flu home to his family.

CHAPTER 17

The Plane Crash

Larry and Jack left the soda shop and sauntered along Hennepin Avenue, enjoying the warm air at the end of April.

Jack threw his arms into the air. "Finally, spring is here!"

Larry grinned. "And the Old Spanish Lady is gone."

"We can ride trolley cars again without being afraid of catching the flu."

"I don't have to wear a mask anymore!" Larry threw his hat into the air, catching it when it came back down.

"And Greg will be coming home from France soon."

Larry gave Jack a playful sock in the arm. "He sure will! He showed that old Kaiser Bill."

Life is good again, Larry thought.

Still, life wasn't the same as it used to be. The flu hadn't only taken people he knew well, like Grandfather Allerton, Violet, and Charlie. The cheerful, freckled clerk who used to wait on them all the time hadn't been at the soda shop today. Mr. Walton, the cheerful man who delivered the milk, would never come whistling up their front walk again. The young man who used to drive the trolley car he and Jack liked to take downtown to see the flickers had died, and the funny man with the handlebar mustache at the meat market, and the policeman who almost caught Jack with the slingshot in the park. It seemed there were people missing everywhere.

Do any of the people in their families feel guilty for giving them the flu? Larry wondered.

A droning sound caught Larry's attention. He shaded his eyes with his hand and peered at the sky. "Look, Jack, a plane! Looks like an army plane."

It wasn't flying very high—about three hundred feet above the ground, Larry guessed—but that was pretty common. Pilots liked to fly low enough to see the city and guide themselves by the buildings, bridges, and other landmarks.

The drone stopped. The plane began sputtering. Larry frowned. "Something's wrong with the engine."

Other people on the street heard the sound of the plane in trouble and stopped to watch, too.

"Come on," Larry urged the pilot. "Get it going again!"

His heart leaped to his throat when the plane started dropping.

"It's coming down!" He grabbed Jack's arm and yanked him toward the street. "Get out of the way!"

"It's coming down!" someone else in the crowd yelled.

"Watch out!"

"She's comin' down!"

People pushed and bumped into each other in their attempts to dash to safety while they watched the mechanical bird dropping from the sky.

It fell slowly, the pilot fighting all the way to get the engine to run right.

"It's going to hit the building! It's going to hit McNutty and Defoe's Auto Firm!" Larry yelled to Jack over the noise of the plane and crowd.

The falling plane caught a trolley line, and the passing trolley rolled to a stop.

The nose of the plane hit the second-story windows above the auto firm. The propeller sent splinters flying like shrapnel. Larry was glad they were far enough away so that the flying glass couldn't hit them.

Horror and fascination kept Larry's gaze glued to the plane. It slowly slid down the wall, past the second-story windows, and through the first-story auto shop windows. The first-story windows ripped the weakened propeller to shreds.

With a crashing thud, the plane settled on the sidewalk. The wings crumpled instantly. Its nose laid in the auto shop window. Its tail was in the street, where it had crumpled a car's front fenders.

"Wow!"

"Have you ever seen the like?"

"Somebody could have been killed!"

Larry ignored the crowd and dashed for the plane. His heart raced. Was the pilot all right?

The young pilot climbed out of the cockpit. He paid no

attention to the crowd. Settling his goggles over his close fitting hat, he looked over his mangled plane.

On the other side of the plane, a passenger climbed out. There was a cut above his right eye. Larry could see that the glass on his broken goggles had cut him.

Beside him, Jack gave a low whistle. "They were pretty lucky to come out of that crash with just one small cut."

Larry walked up beside the pilot. "What happened to your engine?"

The man shrugged, still staring at his plane. "It was acting up a little, but I believe I could have made it back to the airfield if it weren't for the air currents. They sucked us right down. I've been flying out of Fort Snelling all week and haven't had any trouble until today."

The nose of the plane was so hot they couldn't stand too close, but the pilot and his friend peered at it as if they could see right through the crumpled metal. They walked around the plane, hands on their hips, checking out the damage. Larry walked right along with them.

The crowd had surged about the plane, eager to see the damage at close hand. They made room for the pilot as he made his way around his craft.

"Too bad about your plane," Larry said to the pilot.

"It won't be so bad if the engine is all right," the pilot told him. "I won't know how it is until it cools down enough so that I can look at it. The rest can be rebuilt more easily and cheaply than the engine."

"Did you fly in the war?" Larry asked.

"No, wish we had! My friend here and I are cadet pilots. The war was over before we made it to Europe." He stuck out his hand. "My name's Butters."

"Larry Allerton." He shook the pilot's hand. He tried to act grown-up and hoped his excitement didn't show too much!

"You want to fly planes when you grow up, Larry?"

"Yes, sir!"

Pilot Butters grinned at him. "You'll love it, kid. There's nothing like it in the world. If flying is your dream, don't ever give up on it."

A man with a pad and pencil pushed himself between Larry and the pilot. "So what happened? How'd your plane end up in an auto shop on Hennepin Avenue?"

Larry backed away from the reporter. Some adults didn't have any manners! Acted like kids weren't even people. He was glad Uncle Erik didn't act like that when he reported on things for the newspaper.

Larry would probably have stayed around checking out the plane and hoping to talk to the pilots again all night if Jack hadn't finally insisted they leave.

"We're already going to be late for dinner, and the trolley won't be running until they get the electric line fixed. We need to head back."

Larry couldn't get the plane out of his mind. "Did you see the way it hovered against that building? Looked like a bird fluttering against a strong wind."

"Still think you want to fly one day, after seeing that accident?"

"Sure!"

Jack shook his head. "You're pretty brave."

Larry shrugged. "Nobody was hurt. Well, not badly. I didn't see anyone in the crowd who was hurt, either."

"People were just lucky."

"Maybe. Mr. Butters, that's the pilot," he tried to make the comment sound casual, "told me the air currents dragged the plane down. There must be a way to make a plane's engine stronger, don't you think?"

Jack's arms spread wide. "How would I know? I'm just a kid!"

"There has to be. Maybe one day I'll find a way."

"Sure you will. And maybe one day man will fly to the moon."

Larry was disappointed his friend didn't seem to think he was smart enough to help design planes one day. *Mr. Butters said to never give up on my dream,* he reminded himself.

The next day, there was a picture of the airplane and Pilot Butters in the paper, along with an article about the accident. Larry and Jack read every word as they stretched out on the parlor rug at Larry's house.

Some people thought there should be laws saying how low planes could fly over the city. No one had been hurt this time, the article said, but one day someone would be hurt if planes kept flying into buildings.

But the plane crash and everything else was pushed from the newspaper and everyone's thoughts by more important news: The 151st had landed in New York Harbor!

CHAPTER 18

Homecoming

"Greg will be home in less than two weeks!" Jack shouted the news as he raced up the steps to the Allertons' front porch.

Larry and Gloria were sitting on the porch.

"Why does it take so long?" Gloria asked.

Jack dropped to the floor and wrapped his arms around his knees. His eyes sparkled with happiness. "The men have to pass their physicals before they are sent home."

Father walked up the sidewalk, a newspaper under his arm. He grinned at Jack. "It's great to hear Greg and the other boys in the 151st will be home soon. The paper's full of pictures of the regiment in Brooklyn Harbor and interviews with the men.

You and Larry wouldn't be interested in reading them, would you?"

"Well, I guess we would!" Jack grinned back at him.

Father left them with the newspaper and went inside.

There weren't any pictures of Greg, but it was fun to see pictures of men he'd fought beside.

The men had both funny and scary stories to tell. "Listen to this!" Jack read aloud, " 'Minnesota's 151st arrests General.' "

"They arrested a German general? Let me see that!" Larry tugged at the page.

Jack held fast, his gaze glued to the article. "It was during the last day of fighting at Argonne. The Minnesota men thought they were the first Americans in the area. They spotted a man all by himself, wearing the uniform of an American private. They figured he was a spy and arrested him."

"And he was a German general?" Larry asked again.

"No." Jack laughed. "He was an American general. It was General Douglas McArthur."

Larry's jaw dropped. "They arrested General McArthur?"

"He was checking out the area. He was dressed like a private so if the Germans caught him, they wouldn't know who he was."

Larry chuckled. "I guess his disguise worked! Even his own soldiers didn't know him."

Larry liked the article about the regiment's rainbow emblem. He'd known that the 151st was called the Rainbow Division, but he hadn't known how important rainbows had been to the soldiers.

"It says here that rainbows appeared in the sky before some of the 151st's most important battles," he told Jack. "The morning they started for the place where they fought their very first battle there was a rainbow. And before some of their other battles, too. Why, there was even a rainbow while they were going over the top at the start of one battle!"

He looked up from the article. "Kind of reminds you of the story of Noah's ark, doesn't it, and the rainbow God told Noah was a sign of God's promise not to ever destroy the earth like that again?"

Jack nodded. "Maybe the soldiers thought the rainbows were God's promises to them, too."

"Maybe they did."

"I'll be glad when Greg is home and can tell us stories about the war in person," Jack said.

It seemed that everywhere Larry went, everyone was talking about "our boys" returning home. St. Paul and Minneapolis were planning a huge welcome-home celebration. The soldiers' trains would pass through the Minnesota cities on their way to Fort Dodge, so they could only stay one day in each city. After a couple days in Fort Dodge, the soldiers would be coming back to Minneapolis and St. Paul to stay.

In Minneapolis, temporary pillars were being hastily built along Nicollet Avenue. They were to be decorated for a parade. A special grandstand for watching the parade was being built for the families of the soldiers. Larry couldn't help being a little jealous that Jack would be sitting on that grandstand while Larry watched from the crowd along the street!

The night before the soldiers were to be in Minneapolis, Larry stood on the front porch. Through the rain, he stared at Jack and Mabel's houses, standing side by side across the street. When Greg came to Minneapolis tomorrow, Mabel's sister, Violet, wouldn't be there to welcome him back. Sadness and confusion filled Larry's chest at the thought.

Larry heard the front door open and close. A minute later, Father stood beside him, hands in his trousers.

"A big day ahead tomorrow," Father said.

Larry nodded.

"Suppose you'll be going to the parade with the rest of your school chums on the trolleys?"

Larry nodded again.

"Of course, it would be more fun for you if you could go with Jack. I think you'll find it exciting even without him."

Larry nodded one more time.

"Looks like the rain is letting up. Maybe we'll have good weather for the parade tomorrow."

Larry nodded.

"All of Minneapolis has been grinning since they found out the 151st landed in New York Harbor. Want to tell me why you aren't smiling at the thought of seeing Greg and the boys tomorrow, Larry?"

"Well," Larry shifted his weight from one foot to another, trying to get up the courage to tell Father his thoughts. He stared at Mabel and Violet's house.

"When soldiers go to war, everyone knows the soldiers might get killed. Everyone worries about them and wonders which ones will live and which ones will die."

"Yes, that's true."

"No one thought the people at home would die while the soldiers were away fighting the war. But that's what happened. Now lots of parents and wives and brothers and sisters and children and girlfriends like Violet are dead."

Larry felt Father's hand on his shoulder, but Father didn't say anything. He just waited for Larry to continue.

"Jack's family is happy Greg is alive and they will see him

tomorrow, but Father, Greg will be sad because Violet isn't alive."

"I know, Son. Life doesn't seem fair sometimes, does it?"

Larry shook his head. He took a deep, shaky breath. His chest hurt from the pain he'd been keeping in his heart all these months. "And. . .and I almost killed my own mother and brother!"

Father's hand tightened on his shoulder.

Larry almost stopped breathing. He couldn't believe he'd blurted out his secret!

"What in the world are you talking about?" Father asked.

Terror whipped through Larry. If he told, Father might hate him.

"Larry, tell me what you meant."

"I–I. . ." Larry swallowed hard. "I disobeyed you and didn't wear the mask, and I played football when you told me not to, and I went to the train station to see some returning soldiers." The words tumbled out.

"And then I got sick, and then Gloria and Harry and Mother got sick, and Harry and Mother almost died. If they'd died, it would have been because of me."

Father groaned.

Larry bit his bottom lip and stared across the street, not daring to look at him.

"Larry, look at me."

Larry looked at his shoes instead.

Father put a hand on each of Larry's shoulders and turned him until they were facing each other. Larry still didn't look at him.

"We don't know how the flu came to our house, Larry. Remember the jump rope rhyme about the bird named Enza?"

Larry nodded.

"The bird flew into a house on the air. Flu germs are carried on the air, and there's no telling how they came to the people in our house."

Larry dared a glance at him. Hope began to push at the pain in his heart. "Really?"

"Really. One of our family might have picked up the germs from the milkman, or the wood delivery man, or your mother might have picked them up when she did the marketing."

"I. . .I suppose it could have happened that way." Larry glanced up at his father.

"I've felt guilty about the flu sometimes, too," his father said.

"*You,* Father?"

"Oh, yes. I'm a doctor, but try as I did to save them, many of my patients died. I didn't know how to help them. I felt guilty because I didn't know more. I felt guilty that I hadn't been able to protect my family from the flu. I felt guilty because I let you and Gloria go back to school in December. Mother told me there were times she felt guilty, too."

Larry stared at him. "Why would Mother feel guilty?"

"Because she was trying to protect herself and our family from the flu, she couldn't help other families with the flu as much as she would have liked."

"Oh."

"Larry, the Spanish flu wasn't any normal flu. This flu killed more people than were killed in the Great War. It killed more people than were killed in many wars. The Spanish flu caused the worst time of sickness the world has known in six hundred years."

"In over six hundred years?"

"Yes. It was like a plague. The wisest, most knowledgeable people in the world didn't know how to prevent it or how to fight it. You shouldn't have disobeyed, but we don't know that you brought the flu to the family. Even if you did bring it, if you hadn't, there's a very good chance your mother and Harry would have caught it from someone else anyway."

Larry gulped. "Then. . .then you aren't angry at me?"

"No, I'm not angry."

Larry felt better than he'd felt in a long time.

Father pointed to the sky. "Look at that. A rainbow!"

A pallet of colors bridged the spring sky. *God's promise,* Larry thought.

It was with a much lighter heart that Larry joined Gloria and Mabel on the trolley headed from school to the parade the next day.

The sidewalks were so crowded it was impossible to move without stepping on someone's toes or getting an elbow in the ribs, but no one seemed to mind. People sat on window ledges and leaned out of windows and stood on street benches and perched on lamp posts. Flags hung from every window. People wore colorful ribbons around their arms to represent rainbows.

The Minnesota National Guard led the way for the 151st. When the fighting men just returned from France made their way down the crowded street, roars and cheers filled the air until Larry couldn't hear himself cheering. Khaki-dressed soldiers with trench helmets set at a jaunty angle marched down the street with wide grins. A grinning gunner held the leash of the division's famous goat mascot, who trotted alongside the soldiers.

Larry reached as high as he could, waving the small flag he'd brought.

"Well done, men! Welcome home!" he called. He yelled until his throat hurt, and then he yelled some more.

He searched the smiling faces beneath the helmets, hoping for a glimpse of Greg. There! He grabbed Mabel's arm and leaned close to yell in her ear. "There he is! Third one in. See him? It's Greg! He's home!"

Mabel's eyes sparkled with happy tears. She stood on the edge of the curb. "Greg! Welcome home!"

Larry could tell what she was yelling, even though he couldn't hear her.

And then it seemed Greg caught sight of them! He didn't miss a step. He just looked at Mabel and winked. As quickly as he had arrived, he was gone.

Mabel grinned at Gloria and Larry. Larry grinned back. Then they started cheering while the rest of the 151st continued to march by.

The War to End All Wars was over. The Plague of the Spanish Lady was over.

It was a new beginning for the world and Minneapolis, and for Greg and Larry as well. Anything was possible.

There's More!

The American Adventure continues with *Women Win the Vote*. The entire Allerton family is involved in activities to help pass and ratify the amendment that will give women the right to vote.

That is, until Larry gets caught up with the barnstormers. Nothing is more important to him than being with those planes and their pilots. He sneaks away during the day, leaving Gloria and their mother with extra work to do. After his parents punish him, he starts skipping school to spend time at the airfield. Finally he is caught by a truant officer.

Will anything convince Larry that he needs to make time for his family and schoolwork?